14/12/15.

To
x

NIGHT

of the

SHADOW

Dad x
Janet

Happy Christmas!
Hope you enjoy!
This is my MAGNUM OPUS
My longest to date.
Memories of my
childhood in Acton Park
& crossing the infamous
bridge!
Also recalling God's
blessing on my life
& His triumphs over
darkness in the lives of
others.
Dad x

NIGHT *of the* SHADOW

"Even though I walk through the valley of the shadow of death, I will fear no evil..."

(Psalm 23)

PETER GARNER

AuthorHouse™ UK
1663 Liberty Drive
Bloomington, IN 47403 USA
www.authorhouse.co.uk
Phone: 0800.197.4150

Published by AuthorHouse 03/04/2015

ISBN: 978-1-5049-3707-8 (sc)
ISBN: 978-1-5049-3728-3 (e)

Print information available on the last page.

CONTENTS

PART ONE

PART TWO

PART ONE

MYSTERIOUS GOINGS ON IN THE PARK

'The mystery of iniquity is already at work'

(The Bible)

It was the night of the full moon and in the eerie silence dark figures stood around the mystic stone circle. The central figure robed in white raised his hands to the moon, while the rest bowed in reverence. The nearby town was generally fast asleep, all unaware of the secret gathering in the park by the lake. They were oblivious to the evil plans soon to be put into operation. It was the midnight hour on a dark night and the night was growing darker........

Later the next day.........

"The chances of anything coming from Mars are a million to one", he said. "The chances of anything coming from Mars are a million to one – but still they come......."

The haunting strains of Jeff Wayne's musical version of H.G.Wells' WAR OF THE WORLDS echoed round the house. It was a favourite of both James (Bondy) and Mary and having listened to it several times over now they were starting again!

Their parents had introduced it to them and it was an instant hit. It wasn't that they believed in "Little Green Men from Mars" as the saying goes, or giant machines capable of destroying with ease the most sophisticated human weaponry. For them it underlined the important fact that there are things far beyond human reason – things which we can't explain, which can nevertheless be very real.

They believed that the deepest and profoundest things in life have their source outside the capabilities of the human mind – and that applied to both good and evil. Somehow the fantastic music and the compelling narrative conveyed that fact to them even though they didn't go along with the full content and meaning of it all.

The deep, rich, powerful voice of Richard Burton the Welsh actor reverberated once more round the room:

"No one would have believed.....that human affairs were being watched...No one could have dreamed we were being scrutinised across the gulf of space, *as* minds immeasurably superior to ours, slowly and surely drew their plans against us."

Then the dramatic, pulsating music invaded their emotions and fired their imagination.

It was powerful stuff, but they were not gullible youngsters. They were in fact very bright, as their teachers in the Sixth Form would readily testify. But they believed there was a mystery to life and things were rarely just what they seemed.

Then, of course, there was the little matter of the ghost of Judge Jeffreys! James' granddad had recently told him about it and James had told Mary. He remembered the conversation well................

"No I never saw him James, but I knew some who said they had – more than once! On the old bridge they said they saw him. At night of course, when they were crossing the bridge."

Bondy leaned forward as his grandfather spoke.

"Of course", his grandfather continued, "we weren't supposed to cross the bridge, day or night. It was wired off, surrounded by barbed wire all along it. The bridge wasn't safe you see and there were planks missing all the way along. You could end up in the lake. The lake narrowed in that place and this bridge was there and you used to be able to cross. But then they put notices up and the barbed wire." He paused as he pictured how it used to be, shifting his position in his arm chair and giving a little grunt as he did so.

"But did you cross it, even though you weren't supposed to?" asked James smiling and looking him in the eyes.

His granddad's eyes twinkled and he smiled broadly. "Of course we did!"

"But you never saw the ghost of the hanging judge as they called him?"

"No, son, I never saw him. In the 17th century he lived here in the Acton Hall. His grandfather was a judge and George decided that he would follow the same career. At the age of 33 he became the Lord Chief Justice of England and two years later Lord Chancellor. There was this rebellion led by the Duke of Monmouth – he was a Protestant and didn't want a Catholic King on the throne. In fact he felt he was the rightful heir to the English throne rather than James the Second. The rebellion didn't get very far, I'm afraid. Judge Jeffreys was in charge of what became known as the Bloody Assize, when the rebels were brought to trial. It is said that about 200 victims were hung drawn and quartered and many more sent as slaves to the West Indian plantations. So you can see how the Judge got his reputation and how stories of his ghost spread around like some sort of warning to everyone that he still walked the bridge at night."

"People still tell these stories though, don't they, about the hall and the park and the horrible and terrifying things he did?" James grimaced as he thought of the horror of it all.

"Well, of course, the hall and the bridge are no longer there as you well know. His home in Acton Hall was demolished about sixty years ago in the 1950s. There are apartments in a hall built on the site and there are still stories of ghosts around there and in the park."

"Well I don't believe in ghosts, in one sense", said James. "I wouldn't go looking for them – I think that can lead to bad things – but I do think there are evil things that go on that can't be explained."

"You're right James", said his granddad. "But you're not expecting to meet up with the awful judge any time soon?" He laughed as he said it.

"Certainly not!" James replied. *But perhaps he was wrong about that.*

CHAPTER 1

I'VE SEEN THAT GHOST!

It was Harry who said it. Well we all know Harry – a bit too excitable and prone to exaggerate! Still, he was fairly convinced about it and James thought he must have seen something; but, Judge Jeffreys? - no way! They arranged to meet with Harry later in the park.

"Come on then, Harry; show us where you were when you saw this *thing."* James could not hide the scepticism in his voice.

Harry looked at the three friends and his eyes widened in a mixture of fear and excitement as he spoke.

"Look, I've seen a few scary things in my time as you know, but this was different. It's not the same when you're talking ghosts". He paused as he thought about the incident, screwing up his face in concentration.

"Remember, you've showed me that picture out of the history book of that Judge with his wig on and what I saw looked like it - honest it did!"

"But where were you at the time? You couldn't have been on the bridge because there isn't one now." said Toby as he threw a stone into the lake beside which they were all lounging about on the grassy bank.

"Well, it was night time and I was doing my thing – you know wandering about as I do. I know you've told me to try and stop it 'cos I'm supposed to be sleeping at that time in the early hours of the morning. But I am better than I used to be – I just couldn't sleep, so out I went. I was walking past the place where the grounds of the old hall used to be - you know, where the judge used to live. And he just seemed to come out of nowhere. I hid in the trees. Then when I looked, he'd gone, just like he'd vanished into thin air; gone!"

They decided partly out of loyalty to Harry that they would meet that night and investigate.

"I'm not really sure why we're going on this wild goose chase", said James. Mary agreed, but added with a smile; "Perhaps you mean this wild *ghost* chase!"

Toby laughed as they left Harry behind to return to their own homes, adding his own brand of humorous comment with:

"Hey Bondy, if it is a ghost your catapult won't be much good!"

It was a Friday night so they could have a break from school work. James and Mary were in the middle of A level studies, while Toby had pursued a more practical college course relating to car mechanics.

That night they met up with Harry, as arranged, each carrying a torch and feeling both nervous and excited at the same time. The sky was somehow blacker than usual until a bright full moon burst out from behind the clouds as they made their way across the park towards the lake. The moon's reflected light lit up the lake as they approached it with an instinctive caution. They passed the place where the old wooden bridge had once stood. The bridge had of course been removed long before their time, but the memories still lingered around that spot. It was never passed without someone commenting, or making reference to "meeting the judge on the bridge!" The chattering and laughing which had earlier marked their progress towards the lake, now gave way to a solemn and earnest silence. Harry may have been the gullible one among them, but deep down they had a sneaking feeling that there might be something in it – whatever that something was!

A strong wind had suddenly got up and was making weird and eerie whistling noises among the trees that surrounded the park. Like a piper piping a solemn tune, the sound made a strange and haunting accompaniment to their barely audible footsteps across the park.

"It's a bit scary", said Mary in a hoarse whisper, not really sure why she was whispering.

"It's only the wind blowing in the trees", said James who suddenly realised that he was also whispering, for some reason!

"Why are we whispering?" said Toby in an equally hoarse whisper!

There was a pause and then Harry, who up to this point had been silent, joined in:

"I'm the only one who's not whispering!"

Except that he said it in a whisper, which finally caused the bubble of nervous tension to burst and they all started sniggering, holding their hands over their mouths.

They would not have found it all so funny if they had realised that behind some trees just ahead of where they were standing, a pair of eyes was trained on them, watching their every move. A dark figure sunk back into the darkness of the trees as the youngsters approached. His eyes never left them and as they passed by the spot where he was, he smiled grimly to himself and began, stealthily, to follow them.

In ten minutes or so the foursome were approaching the area where the famous old hall had once stood. Here and there were reminders of the past, despite the absence of any old ruins left behind. There was just something about the place that made them conscious of its infamous owner and there must have been at least some ancient trees that would have witnessed the presence of the Judge and his family.

"Just here!" said Harry. "It was just here. I was up near those trees when I saw it."

Suddenly there was a noise behind them and they spun round in horror just in time to see a black cat racing from the undergrowth and scampering up the field and finally out of sight. They shone their torches into the undergrowth, instinctively feeling that someone may have disturbed the cat. They held their breath and waited in silence, hearts beating fast – but nothing stirred except for the wind rustling the leaves in the trees. The eyes that had observed them before were still watching them, but the sinister figure could not be seen, being well hidden behind the trees.

They stood looking at the old island which lost its island status when the lake dried up and the water receded. They had often played games there when they were younger. They still did occasionally – or at least messed about, when tensions at school got too much! Now, somehow, the scene took on a deeply sinister appearance and the shadows cast by the brightness of the moon gave a truly ghostly feeling to the place.

"Well, whatever it was you saw, it's not here now", said James who was beginning to feel he'd rather they moved on and got back home. "Shall we go? Is that ok Harry? We've had a look now and there's clearly nothing here."

"Yeah, I guess you're right", said Harry, looking a little disappointed in one sense and a little relieved in another. The other two nodded in agreement and they all turned and began to make their way back towards the lake.

Toby and Harry set off in the lead, while James and Mary followed behind them. James leaned over towards Mary and spoke in a whisper.

"To be honest, ghost or not, I felt sure we were being watched and whoever it was, I don't think for a minute, that they were friendly. Maybe something is going on around here!"

The eyes that watched from behind the trees followed their progress till they disappeared from view. Instantly a dark figure moved out from his hiding place, took out his mobile phone, dialled a number and began a long conversation. When he had finished he disappeared into the trees again as the moon also disappeared behind a black cloud.

CHAPTER 2

HAMMY HAMSTER

Monday, and it was history with "Hammy". Mr Hamilton the history teacher was not a favourite with James and Mary, or the rest of the class for that matter. They were both doing the subject for A level - they found it really interesting. They were especially enthusiastic about aspects of local history, but their enthusiasm was waning under the influence of "Hammy". He had taken over part way through the term on account of the enforced retirement, due to ill health, of their favourite history teacher. His name was Mr Davies – fondly known - on account of his first name, as Granny. His first name was Granville and he was a big round-faced Granddad of a man, which meant that Granny was not quite appropriate. However Granny it was and he was just about the most popular teacher in the school.

Granny had inspired them as well as amused them. He had the habit, especially as he got older of mixing his words up. So, for example, instead of telling them he would "dictate some notes" to them, he would say that he would, "dict*ote* some *nates*"! During the dictation he would often get mixed up whilst emphasising the correct punctuation and say, "two dats and a dosh", instead of "two dots and a dash"! But although they laughed, they also recognised his wonderful way of teaching history and they were really sad when he had to retire.

So now it was Hammy! His full title when the pupils were feeling particularly bored with his lessons, was "Hammy hamster"! This was quite appropriate for a number of reasons. In a funny sort of way, he did look a little like a hamster. He was, in contrast to dear old "Granny", a thin weed of a man, which in itself hardly gave him hamster-like characteristics. But he did have a rather sharply pointed face, which could be construed as hamster-like – and was, very quickly, by the pupils.

However it was not so much his build but rather his way of walking which caused them to label him with the hamster description. When he entered the room he seemed to sort of "scurry" into it with quick little steps, which reminded them of a hamster on a wheel. In their mind's eye they could just imagine him on a hamster wheel pedalling away and yet, getting nowhere fast, which was what his history lessons often felt like. One of the pupils had come up with the amusing comment that: "He'd better not go on the London Eye – they'd never get him off!"

Other pupils thought of him as a male version of "Keyhole Kate" from the popular comic. Apart from being thin and weedy with a sort of pinched face ending in a pointed nose, he was also, rather short-sighted. He wore glasses with thick lenses, perched on the end of his protruding peninsular of a nose, through which peered large staring eyes. Into the bargain he had very large ears, which seemed strangely, to give him stereophonic hearing powers. He seemed capable of hearing the slightest whisper in the classroom. This also led to the comment by the pupils regarding his ears: "All, the better to hear you with, my dear!" Suddenly the hamster had turned into a wolf! Although "Keyhole Kate" was popular for a while, it was ultimately "Hammy" that won the day.

He was certainly very knowledgeable and well qualified in his subject – he just couldn't make it very interesting and the pupils in the history class struggled.

"What are we going to do today, I wonder?" said James to Mary as they made their way to the history lesson.

"I think we're due to do Caradoc, or Caractacus, as the Romans called him – one of our famous Welsh ancestors, of course." she replied.

"At least we don't have to do Latin", said James in response to the mention of the Latin name for Caradoc. "Remember that rhyme my granddad told me he used to say, when he was in school?

Latin is a language as dead as dead can be,
It killed the ancient Romans and now it's killing me!

Mary laughed, but pointed out that the Romans had contributed so much to our language and Latin was still used for medical terms and for the classification of plants. "So maybe it still lives on!" James nodded in agreement and they carried on to their appointment with Hammy, which turned out to be not so bad after all.

Later on after lessons were over they were cycling home together when they came across Toby, also on his way home. He beckoned to them and they pulled up for a chat. His face showed considerable concern.

"What's up Tobe?" said James, noticing the anxious look on his normally cheerful face.

"I've only just heard", he said; "though apparently others have known for some weeks. There are a number of youngsters off the estate who have been missing and although it happens from time to time it seems different from before. You know, they often turn up after a week or longer. Maybe they've fallen out with their parents, or perhaps worse, there's been stuff happening – violence by their father and they can't stand any more. There's loads of reasons for it as you well know, both of you. I left home in the past myself, when I started messing with drink and drugs and stuff; but somehow this seems different. It doesn't fit any of the usual patterns of behaviour. Some of the youngsters come from happy homes – it's weird!

"Are the police onto it?" asked Mary.

"Yes", replied Toby grimly. "Apparently they've been investigating for some weeks now but with no break-through at all."

"I wonder if Harry has come across anything – apart from his supposed meeting with the famous ghost of Judge Jeffreys?" James was recalling the fact that in the past Harry had discovered vital information with his night-time and early morning wanderings and eaves-droppings. It was a habit he had picked up in the past, when he had wandered in the night trying to escape his brutal father.

"Maybe we should ask him", said Toby.

"Maybe what he saw was nothing to do with ghosts, but rather something even more sinister", said Mary.

They decided to do just that. Harry had a nose for secret goings on and maybe he was onto something already without realising it. Maybe he had seen or heard other things which might be significant.

That night in the park, at the spot where the four youngsters had gone ghost - hunting, a strange, ghostly figure appeared out of the trees and stood for a while, listening. Then he suddenly turned and disappeared into the bushes and trees.

As if from nowhere, two more figures appeared - they also stood as if listening. They too had a ghostly appearance, for though they were actually dressed in black from head to toe, their faces stood out so white in the blackness of the night that it gave off a frightful, eerie, ghostly light. To an observer they would have seemed like some sort of unearthly presence from another planet. Then as they walked away and disappeared into the darkness it seemed as if two shining, white faces were walking bodiless across the park. They were making for the ancient-looking stone circle which stood at the top of the grassy bank. It represented a Druid's Circle.

CHAPTER 3

THE NEW LIBRARIAN!

There was a new librarian at the local library and all the boys had suddenly become avid readers of books. She was a good-looking lady in her early thirties – though you could have taken her for a sixth former in the school. Many of the boys in the sixth form and lower down the school, for that matter, probably wished that she was just that, but unfortunately for them all they had was their dreams and fantasies. She was quite tall – especially in her high heels – and of very generous proportions in all the right places! She always dressed smartly in white blouse and closely fitting skirt. She was also extremely pleasant and helpful and seemed to have time for the pupils from school. She realised, of course, that not all the problems in finding books which seemed to beset the male students, were truly genuine. She knew how to send them packing when she needed to get on with her work! But they all loved her. She'd been there now for about six months. *Unfortunately for the star-struck boys, she was married!*

She was called Carol and James and Mary knew her quite well. She had been coming to their local church since she arrived in the area. Toby was fairly smitten with her! They went to the library to do research in their different subjects; James and Mary for their history – particularly local history - and Toby for his car mechanics. The day after their meeting with Toby and their discovery of the strange disappearances on the estate, they called at the library after school. Toby often joined James and Mary because he needed extra encouragement with his college course. All three of them arrived at the library in the centre of town, parking their bikes in the place provided.

As they entered the library, they noticed a man engaged in earnest conversation with Carol, the librarian, near the local history section. James and Mary were heading for that particular section, but when they arrived the man seemed to lower his voice and ushered the lady away to another corner of the large room. He was a tall skinny man with a thin moustache and a bald head. He was wearing a large flowing black overcoat, which hardly seemed appropriate for the time of year and the prevailing temperature in the library. On his feet he wore brightly polished black shoes, while in his right hand he carried a beautifully carved, ornate walking stick. In his other hand, to complete the outfit, was a black trilby hat, which he had removed whilst addressing the lady librarian. He was in many ways the image of the perfect gentleman.

"I don't like the look of him", said James.

"Neither do I", replied Mary. "Not quite what he seems".

They both craned their necks to see exactly where the two of them had gone and strained their ears to try and catch what was being said. They could see them but could hear nothing. However it was clear that Carol was agitated and that the man was annoyed about something. He suddenly turned abruptly on his heel and left the building, his long black overcoat billowing out slightly, indicating the speed at which he was travelling and the angry mood that was clearly driving him along. The two youngsters quickly made their way towards the librarian who was visibly upset.

"Hey, Carol, it's none of our business, but we couldn't help noticing how unpleasant that man was with you!" James lowered his voice in keeping with the general policy of quietness within the confines of the library.

Carol smiled as she responded; "I know James, it's a mystery to me. He's on about some manuscript or other that he thinks we have here, relating to the old hall and Judge Jeffreys. But I know nothing about it. I've not been here that long, as you know. He's asked me before and I've told him that I'll find out if I can, but nothing has turned up, so I can't help him."

"Why does he want it, do you know?" asked Mary.

"Oh it's something to do with research he's doing about the old hall and its history – he's a history scholar or something and it's very important to him."

"Well he's no need to get like that about it", said James.

The librarian smiled at them, thanking them for their concern and then reminding them she had work to do, she quickly clickety-clicked her way back to her desk on her high heels, leaving a waft of sweet-smelling perfume in her wake.

"Mmm, I must find out what that perfume is and get some – if I can afford it", said Mary.

"Yes, it is rather nice", said James, "but I like you as you are."

He took hold of her hand and led her to the history section where they eventually found the books they were looking for. They left the building holding hands, giving a wave to Carol as they passed the desk.

Suddenly James stopped in his tracks. "Where's Toby? I've completely forgotten about him."

To their surprise Toby appeared from around the corner of the library, clearly out of breath and full of excitement.

"I followed him", he said, breathlessly, "and you'll be very interested to know where he went."

"Where who went?" said James looking puzzled.

"You know, The Thin Man, that's what I call him – the one in the big black overcoat." Toby was grinning as he spoke, but then his face became deadly serious. "He looks a bit suspicious to me."

"We agree", said Mary, "but we didn't realise you had seen him."

"Oh come on, I haven't spent all this time with Bondy here without getting a nose for suspicious characters!"

The other two grinned and then Bondy asked Toby what had actually happened.

Toby told them that he had been looking unsuccessfully for a particular book to do with his college course, when he realised that Carol, the librarian was close by.

"I could smell that lovely perfume", he said, his eyes rolling round in his head in comic imitation of some kind of Rudolf Valentino romantic.

"Then I heard the voice of *Thin Man*! He sounded really angry and I felt like going round the other side and punching him on the nose. Well, of course I didn't do that – I am trying now to keep that sort of thing for the boxing ring, as you know. But I could see through the gaps in the book shelf that they were just the other side of where I was standing and I didn't like what I was hearing."

He told them that he had heard the stuff about the special manuscript and how keen he was to get it, "being a historian and all that."

"And then I peered through the gap between the books and saw the look on his face. I felt a bit like I did when I saw *The Man with the Crooked Face* – you remember that, of course?"

They remembered it well!

"So I decided to follow him when he went out."

"Where did he go?" Mary and James chorused in total harmony.

"Well, he went outside the library and walked for a few yards; then he paused and took something out of his pocket – like a slip of paper or something. It must have had an address on it. He studied it and then walked on till he came to the right turn where those rather nice houses are – sort of Victorian-looking. He walked down the street looking at the numbers; then he stopped at one of them and rang the door bell. A man came to the door and they stood and chatted for a while. *Thin Man* took what seemed like a card from his pocket, the other man looked at it, smiled and let him in. Then I came back here to tell you."

James and Mary looked puzzled; then James broke the silence:

"But you said we'd be interested to know where he went. I don't understand."

"I'm in the dark too", said Mary.

"Well, get this", said Toby, a look of triumph on his face. "Guess who opened the door?"

"Frankenstein's monster!" said James, grinning rather impatiently.

"No", replied Toby, "It was dear old Granny Davies, your old history teacher!"

James looked at Mary and Mary looked at James; then they both looked back at Toby.

"Now *that is* interesting!" said James, while Mary simply stared incredulously.

Then she spoke out strongly: "But they just don't fit; they're as different as chalk and cheese, as my dad would say."

"On the other hand", responded James, "what they do have in common is the fact that they are historians."

"And", said Mary gesturing with her finger for emphasis, "Granny is chairman of the local history society."

"Correct", said James. "And no doubt he would have been asking Granny about that manuscript."

"Okay, but that's all they *do* have in common", said Toby emphatically.

The trio walked away to gather their bikes, still shaking their heads and chattering about the incident, occasionally stopping and facing one another to make another point in the argument. Then they mounted their bikes and sped off down the road.

In the old Victorian house the two historians were deep in conversation and Mr Davies (Granny) was thoroughly enjoying the chance to talk with someone who almost matched his own knowledge of the local history. The visitor – now clearly labelled by Toby as *Thin Man* – was particularly interested in Granny's knowledge of Judge Jeffreys and the old hall in the park. He was sitting on the edge of his seat, his piercing black eyes boring into the gentler blue of Granny's eyes.

It was clear the subject matter was of the greatest importance to him, while Granny sat back in his arm chair obviously thoroughly enjoying himself.

But was there more to it than that?

CHAPTER 4

THAT'S NO GHOST!

By the weekend the mystery – if it was a mystery – regarding Granny and the Thin Man, was almost forgotten. Anyway Harry was still bothered about his other mystery – the ghost of Judge Jeffreys. They decided, again out of loyalty to Harry, that they ought to have another try to sort out what it was in the park that Harry saw, if he really saw anything at all.

Also, James still remembered the feeling he had shared with Mary that somehow they had been watched.

They had special permission from parents to stay at Toby's place which was nearer to the park. Toby's mum and dad were a little more lenient regarding bedtime hours and turned a blind eye to the fact that they would probably be out after midnight. Well it was the weekend – so no school in the morning. She loved having them anyway.

They set off, armed with torches and some bags of crisps and a few bars of chocolate in case they got peckish. It was a fresh spring evening and the park was bathed in silence as they approached the lake and the site of the old bridge. *No sign of Judge Jeffreys!* But still the little shiver down the spine was experienced by them all – especially Harry. Yes, and they were all talking in whispers, that is if they talked at all. They made their way round the edge of the lake and proceeded onto the other side and finally to the area they had visited on the previous occasion. Exactly on cue an owl hooted and they all looked at each other with a slightly nervous smile.

"All we need is that black cat to come running past", whispered Toby with a grin.

The cat duly ran past and made them all gasp in a mixture of shock and amazement! *What next – the ghost of Judge Jeffreys?* They didn't seriously think so. They must have disturbed the cat as they did on the previous occasion – probably its favourite night-time hunting ground.

On reaching the bushes close to the old island, they paused as Harry – in the lead at this point, anxious to get the first sighting of the ghost – lifted his hand motioning them to stop. Amazingly, in spite of hooting owls and dashing black cats, they had all remained extremely quiet. Harry put his finger to his lips and pointed to the area beyond the bushes. He was onto something. He indicated to them that he would move forward towards the bushes, his sense of responsibility about the whole ghost business lending him courage in spite of his fears, He was just about to disappear round the corner, when to the horror of the on-looking rearguard, an arm reached out and pulled him into the bushes.

The three friends watched, at first stunned into silence, the more so because apart from the threshing sound of a struggle they could hear no sound from Harry. Not knowing what else to do, they simply ran forward to the area where Harry had disappeared, shouting and yelling at the tops of their voices. Rounding the corner of the bush-lined pathway they saw Harry struggling in the arms of a huge man, dressed in what looked like a large, white, long-sleeved shirt and apparently white pyjama trousers. He had long silvery-grey hair down to his shoulders. He also had his hand over Harry's mouth.

Everybody stood still except for Harry, who was struggling in vain to free himself. The strange looking man finally let go of Harry as he realised that the youngsters hardly posed a threat of any sort. The tension eased and James blurted out as he put two and two together:

"That's no ghost, it's a tramp!"

Suddenly the whole scene changed as the man realised exactly what was going on. He let go of Harry, scratched his head, smiled and said:

"I see, so you're doing some ghost hunting are you?"

Then he turned to Harry. "Hey I'm sorry, young feller, never would have been so rough if I'd known you was a young kid. Got kids of me own, you know, God bless'em, but I've lost touch with them now."

He turned to James with a twinkle in his eye: "And less of the tramp! You're not supposed to call me that now, you know. I'm one of them homeless vagrants and it's an infringement of my human rights. I'll have the European Convention on you!"

He burst out laughing, pointing at the bewildered youngsters, until the laughter gave way to a bout of chesty coughing, which finally ended with a trumpet-like blowing of his nose on a filthy rag which he fished out of his pocket.

"Ah that's better", he said, smiling, as James found his tongue again.

"We're really sorry sir, to have disturbed you, only we didn't know you were there and, yes we were ghost hunting. In fact it seems to me that you are the ghost that Harry there thought he had seen the other night."

The friendly giant of a tramp – or vagrant – had put his arm round Harry, who now seemed quite calm and was looking at his erstwhile enemy with something between admiration and amazement.

"As you see I'm no ghost!" Then his face became deadly serious. "I tell you what though; there's been some strange goings on around 'ere, and one reason I was so violent towards the young gentleman 'ere..." He paused and apologised profusely to Harry once more, forgetting he had already done it. Then he continued: "Now where was I, oh yes, there's been some strange goings on around 'ere and that's why I defended myself, 'cause I thought you was someone else. I thought you was them white-faced men in black."

He paused again to let it sink in; then continued after clearing his throat loudly.

"Oh yes, I've seen them alright and I'm not pretendin' I aren't scared, 'cause I am and I'm telling you they're up to no good and that's putting it mildly. I 'ate to think what they're up to. It's weird it is, real weird!"

Mary, James, Toby and Harry looked at one another in astonishment. *What on earth was going on? What was he talking about? What did it mean? Perhaps he'd had a bit too much to drink and was seeing things.*

"Can you explain exactly what you mean by these white-faced men in black, as you call them? What are they, when have you seen them and where have you seen them?" Mary expressed the puzzlement of them all.

They sat down on a park bench and Duke – for that was his name, or at least what everyone called him – began his explanation.

"Now then, I can't give you no exact explanation, as you say, 'cause there's nothing exact about it. And as for who or what they are, don't ask me! They could be anything – like off another planet for all I know. They seem to appear around 'ere." - He pointed to the area around which they were sitting by the old island – "and up there near the circle of stones which goes back 'undreds of years for all I know."

"It's funny you should say that, but when we came here the other night, I was convinced someone was watching us." James voiced what they had all felt that night.

"I only know what my eyes saw," said Duke, "and what they saw was these men – if they was men – all in black, head to toe and their faces all bright white, like luminous and ghostly. I think they seen me and I had to run for it 'cause I reckon they wasn't playing no games. 'Once bitten twice shy' as they say, so I've been careful and though I've seen them a couple of times I've been 'idden away and I don't think they've seen me." He looked at the four astonished youngsters and then after a pause, he scratched his large nose and continued:

"Look you guys, 'ow about we 'elp each other. I reckon you four are as keen as I am to sort this out. It's been the last few months, you see. I was fine till then and then these things started 'appening and my peaceful little spot 'ere where I bed down, not doin' no one no 'arm, it gets invaded by these weird apparitions or whatever they are. 'What's goin' on?' you ask; well I wish I knew."

They parted company after promising to keep in touch. Duke, delighted to have made some young friends who didn't poke fun at him or throw stones and the youngsters pleased to feel that Duke – who was such a great character – took them seriously and was keen to maintain contact.

One or two things were now clearer:

1) Obviously, as he was now prepared to admit, Harry's sighting of the dreaded Judge had actually been a sighting of Duke! He realised that the white shirt and white pyjamas plus the long silvery – grey hair had given the appearance of a ghost in a judge's wig!
2) The strange 'presence' they had felt that night in the park had not been a figment of their imagination. Something *was* going on!

But who were the strange 'Men in Black with White Faces'? They had not met up with Judge Jeffreys, but what dark horror had they unearthed?

CHAPTER 5

LET'S GO AND SEE OLD GRANNY!

The four friends arrived back at Toby's full of excitement and also, to some extent, of apprehension. What had they got themselves into? Who or what were these ghostly *Men in Black*? What were they doing and what was it about the place that served Duke as a home that drew them to it and made them clearly violent towards anyone hanging around? Those questions buzzed around in their minds like busy bees, along with the issue involving the *Thin Man* and his visit to old Granny Davies. Then James hit on an idea.

"Look, why don't we go and visit old Granny? For a start we're still mystified about his recent strange visitor and for another thing, being an expert in local history, might he know something about the hall, the park and the infamous Judge Jeffreys that could explain what is going on?"

They retired to bed and slept on quite late the next day, but soon revived as they smelt the bacon and eggs which Toby's mum was cooking for them!

"You young people need a good breakfast inside you, that's what I always say. Come on down before it gets cold."

They responded with alacrity, the sound of four pairs of feet thundering down the stairs, eloquent testimony to the power of her culinary skills.

The meal was devoured with similar alacrity and washed down with cups of steaming hot tea supplied with fresh buttered toast and marmalade.

Breakfast over; they lost no time in phoning their old history teacher.

He was in and would be delighted to see them to discuss – as they put it – local history matters. They duly arrived on their bikes in about twenty minutes and were soon ringing the door bell. The door opened to reveal a white-haired, balding, cuddly-looking man in his mid-sixties. He beamed when he saw them.

"Fancy coming to see your old history teacher," he said; the delight on his face evident for them all to see. "This is indeed a treat and brings back an awful lot of memories for me."

There followed a prolonged period, first of introductions – Toby and Harry, who had not been in his class – then of general chatter about how his retirement was going and how they were doing in school and various bouts of laughter over some of the things that had happened in the past.

Then he asked them what it was they had particularly come to see him about.

"As a matter of fact, before you answer that question," he said, - interrupting James as he was about to respond – "you're not the first visitors I've had asking about local history. A gentleman came a few days ago and we had a very interesting conversation about Judge Jeffreys and the lost manuscript relating to the old hall and other various matters. He was very knowledgeable himself about local history, but wondered if I could help him further."

The four youngsters looked at one another knowingly and then James spoke out:

"And did you help him sir?"

The old historian looked at James quizzically and smiled.

"Well, maybe I helped him a little bit, but not too much."

"May we know why that was, sir? I hope you don't mind us asking but we have already met the gentleman and we were not too keen on his manner. Forgive me sir for expressing my opinion so strongly but..."

"Not at all, young James, or should I call you Bondy?" he said with a twinkle in his eye. "I wonder; did you know he had been here to see me?"

When Bondy nodded, somewhat bashfully, he smiled and said:

"It doesn't surprise me at all; don't forget I was there in the school assembly several years ago now, when a certain thirteen year old boy was cheered onto the stage after that famous adventure in the cave. So tell me what really brought you here to see me?"

James told him about the incident in the library and Toby's discovery of the mysterious stranger's visit to the history teacher's house. The others chipped in as they described the incidents down at the old hall and the park. They also told him about their new-found friend Duke.

He leaned back in his chair and surveyed the four earnest young faces gazing at him in expectation.

"I have my suspicions too, you know, as you may well have guessed from my earlier remarks. I actually enjoyed our conversation at first – he is clearly well qualified in the historical field and we had much in common. However my suspicions were raised when I was able to confirm to him that though the manuscript he sought was not in my possession, I had seen it and could recall much that was in it."

He went on to tell them that at that point the so-called *Thin Man* had said he would like him to meet with some friends who were also interested in the contents of the manuscript and who would pay him handsomely for the information.

"That's when I smelt a rat," he said, "as you might well expect."

He shook his head and looked deadly serious. "Paying money? What's that all about, I ask you?"

"What do you think is going on sir?" asked Mary, "and do you think it could have anything to do with the strange events at the island and what Duke told us?"

"I really don't know, Mary, I wish I did. You see the manuscript that I saw had a piece missing, so even if I could remember what I *did* read, I never read the whole text. That's the problem."

"Does he know that you didn't see the whole manuscript?" asked James.

"No, I thought I'd keep that little piece of information to myself." replied Granny with a grin. "And, of course, I declined his offer to meet with his friends. I didn't fancy that at all!"

"Is there any chance you might be able to find out more about the missing piece of manuscript? Toby asked, speaking for the first time.

"Well, you never know," he replied smiling again. "I'll be meeting with the local historical society soon and maybe someone there might come up with something. If I do find anything I'll let you know."

The four youngsters left the house after some fond "goodbyes" and promises to call again, especially if the teacher found out any more about the manuscript. They mounted their bikes and rode off down the road heading for Toby's. They did not notice a shadowy figure lurking in the trees across the way from Granny's house. He was wearing a long black overcoat and carried an ornately carved walking stick. *Thin Man* had been observing the house for some time. He climbed into a black car and could be seen instructing the driver to follow the youngsters as they pedalled along. When they arrived at Toby's the car, some distance away, pulled up and inside, the man in the black overcoat could be seen noting down the address in a diary.

He spoke to the man in the front who was driving the car. The man nodded, turned round and said something in response. There was a grim, menacing look on the faces of both men as they carefully turned the car round and sped off in the other direction. What had they said? Why had they followed them anyway? Why were they so keen to get the information about the manuscript? What were they now planning to do? The four youngsters inside Toby's house were all unaware of the presence of the Thin Man in the black overcoat. The sky above had darkened and it began to rain heavily, while from inside the house they heard a rumble of thunder.

CHAPTER 6

THE THIN MAN

The black saloon car sped away from Toby's estate and continued for some time, till the town was left behind and the busy main road gave way to a quiet country lane. They reached a wooded area and pulled into a lay-by; there the car stopped and the engine was switched off. For a while there was silence and then the man in the black overcoat spoke:

"I don't like it; they need watching, I think they could be a nuisance – or maybe even worse than that. They definitely need watching. I saw them in the library. Why did they go to see the old historian? Perhaps he was their teacher, but I rather feel there was more to it than that." He paused and then continued:

"I'm making you responsible, Higgins," he said, addressing the driver of the car. "I want them watched day and night. Report to me each night; you know how to contact me." He leaned forward towards the driver who was half turned towards where he was sitting in the back seat, his piercing black eyes fixed on the man's face. "Don't let me down Higgins, it could turn out badly for you – you understand?"

"Yes boss, I understand", he replied.

Thin Man lifted his ornate walking stick and pressed the point of it against the man's neck, pushing him backwards towards the window of the car. He winced with pain, his eyes staring; wide open with fear.

"Yes boss, honest, you can trust me, I won't let you down!"

"Good, well done Higgins. I'm sure you realise that there are great rewards for success, but also heavy punishments for failure!"

"Yes boss."

Minutes later the car pulled out of the lay-by and proceeded along the wooded country lane. It continued for a few miles and then turned off up a long tree-lined driveway till it reached the elegant frontage of a splendid stone-built mansion. There was a large area for parking in front of stone steps which led up to an ornately carved, huge doorway. The man in the black overcoat got out, ascended the steps, rang the bell and entered as the door was opened by a smartly dressed butler.

The driver turned the car round and drove down the lane, disappearing from the view of the house, behind the trees along the drive. The face at the window watching him was wreathed in a mocking smile. He had removed his black overcoat, but black was still the dominant colour of the suit underneath. Beneath the clothing he wore it was evident that an equally black heart was beating and the squinting look in the black eyes conveyed something dark, evil, terrible. Yet still he smiled as he turned away from the window, poured himself a glass of wine and sat down in a plush arm chair, his legs crossed, while one foot swung nonchalantly up and down as if in harmony with some familiar tune playing in his head.

The magnificent building had three stories and at the apex of one of the pointed roofs, a tiny, slim, slit of a window could be seen. What could not be seen from the ground, except perhaps with a pair of pretty strong binoculars, was the face of a young man peering anxiously out across the grounds of the property. If an observer had been able to look inside the room which the young man occupied, he would have noted that there were three other young men in the room. They all had one thing in common – they were tall and well built and about fifteen years of age.

The room was very large and equipped with table tennis tables, snooker tables and various other leisure facilities including a large screen television set. There was no telephone or computer present and it was clear that the young men had no mobile phones of any sort. The keen observer would have deduced this from the simple fact that none of them were ever seen playing games or making text messages or phone calls.

There was a large dining table and on it the remnants of what had clearly been a substantial meal. Numerous empty cans of beer or lager lay strewn about the table and in some cases, the floor. At the other end of the room were quite lush easy chairs and around the walls, book cases filled with any number of books of all kinds. The occupants were clearly well provided for; they lacked for nothing. Except of course for one thing – *their freedom!*

Why were they here? What was going to happen to them? They did not know; they had not been told. The first week had been great, with plenty of booze and time to laze around, play games or watch TV. They had been promised many other things, with a prosperous future before them – none of them had materialised. It had sounded wonderful – so far it wasn't, in fact it was far from it. It was also clear that they were not free to leave. The place was heavily guarded. Now fear had set in and they realised they had been taken for a ride. That of course was literally true! The black saloon car had brought them there!

They were at the age where they were keen to experiment, to dare to do the unexpected, to rebel, to take a risk. They probably thought in their own way that they could move the world. Of course the famous Archimedes once said that if he was given a place to stand, he could move the world. I suppose being a brilliant scientist and mathematician he had worked out that according to the laws of physics what he said would be possible. The man was a genius! Sadly these young men had not found a place to stand in any sense of that term. They had no sure foundation to their lives and now what little foundation they did have was crumbling beneath them.

Meanwhile, downstairs, *Thin Man* knew what was going to happen to them. He needed fit, strong young men to fulfil his plans. But they also needed to be gullible young men who could be easily led with false promises. They would have to work hard, but they would be well paid and there would be other rewards. But, of course, they would have to be loyal. Disloyalty would not be tolerated. Higgins knew that and they would have to learn it. But it was not yet the right time; other things had to fall into place.

The telephone rang and he picked it up:

"Yes", he replied to the question put to him, "so far, so good. No I do not think there is a real chance of luring *them* into the plan. They're a bit too smart, unfortunately.

There will be other ways of dealing with them and those ways will be pursued at the right time. The timing is vital, as you say. Higgins is watching them and will report to me daily. Yes, three young men and a girl. Yes....Yes....that's right. The manuscript is the crucial thing. I am dealing with it – yes, urgently. Ah yes, the visitor, I keenly await his arrival"

He put the phone down and took another sip of the wine, smiling again to himself. He rang the bell and in no time the smartly dressed butler appeared.

"Yes sir?" he enquired in his usual solemn manner.

"There will be another visitor tonight, Bates. See to it that all appropriate arrangements are made and bring me one of my best wines from the cellar. You know the sort of thing."

"Yes sir, of course sir, I will see to it at once sir."

And with a slight bow, he left the room. Everywhere was silent except for the loud ticking of the large grandfather clock which stood in the corner of the room.

"The timing is vital", he had said.

The clock was ticking loudly!

CHAPTER 7

WHERE'S DUKE?

It was Sunday and the four youngsters arrived at their local church eagerly awaiting the joyous proceedings. "Church" may not have seemed an appropriate way of describing where they met and what they did. The building was in fact a former warehouse just outside the estate; they didn't sit in regimented rows of pews, staring at the backs of one another's necks, but rather on comfortable chairs, in a sort of semi-circle, where most of the time, they could see one another's faces. Church, after all is people, not a building.

Yes there was a lot of noise - in keeping with the psalmist's instruction to "make a joyful noise to the Lord", but equally there were times of profound silence when you could almost hear a pin drop as people felt the presence of a God who was not just a theory from a text book. Often then, the only sound you could hear was the sound of people weeping and the silent prayers of those who knelt beside them to comfort them.

The first time Harry dared to venture in he said:

"It can't be a church, everybody's too happy!"

Toby had been overwhelmed by the strong feeling of love that seemed to envelop him and had commented:

"If this is what God's like, I'm having some!"

The place was used a lot by the community as a whole and it became a centre for all kinds of help to anyone who needed support, care and advice. It was 'open house' on Sunday and many wandered in who would not normally darken the doors of most churches. Starting and finishing times were fairly relaxed anyway and they were not frowned upon but welcomed. They were not required to conform to middle class ways of dressing or talking. There was a realisation that in Jesus' day it was the religious people who had criticised Him and eventually had Him crucified. They remembered that He had spent most of His time, not just with His disciples, but with those who were considered 'outsiders'. But in His presence they felt accepted and loved, not scrutinised. He was their friend.

There were lots of young people there, but also lots of older ones too – a balanced combination of enthusiasm and wisdom. The youngsters loved it and didn't have to be dragged there reluctantly by over-zealous parents. In some cases the youngsters had introduced their parents to the church.

On this occasion after the meeting was over, they each went to their respective homes, arranging to meet up in the afternoon by the lake at the park. James had suggested that since they hadn't heard anything from Duke, it might be a good idea to try to find him and share the things they had discovered. So at 2.30 pm they turned up at the park.

They spent a fruitless afternoon searching for Duke. His usual spot seemed to have been abandoned and eventually they reluctantly gave up the search, thinking that they might have more luck at night. James and Mary in particular spent the rest of Sunday afternoon and the evening catching up on some much needed study and project work. They had agreed to meet at nine o' clock when it was just getting dark.

Making their way round past the site of the old bridge, they went through the now familiar ritual of whispering to one another, usually followed by a bout of restrained sniggering when they realised they'd done it again! *The other thing that was repeated, unknown to them of course, was the watching eyes following their every step, peering in the darkness through the trees. Higgins, doing his job perhaps?*

Once again they reached the spot where they had first met Duke and according to a pre-arranged signal, flashed a torch three times. They waited, but there was no response, so they proceeded round the corner and into the bushes where Duke had made his dwelling place. Since there had been no response from him they were not surprised that he was not there. They were disappointed and also somewhat alarmed. Had the white-faced *Men in Black* got him?

"I'm not sure about this", said James, frowning as he spoke. "Somehow it just doesn't fit."

"He could just be out and about", said Mary. "After all tramps, sorry vagrants, don't normally keep regular hours, do they?"

"I'm with Bondy here", said Toby. "Something seems wrong."

"Me too", said Harry, pulling a miserable face. "I hope nothing's happened to him, I really like him."

They scouted around in the bushes for a while hoping to find some sort of clue – anything at all – that might tell them something about what might have happened.

"There's no sign of a struggle." James said.

Then Mary let out a little gasp of surprise. She had been looking further back into the bushes beyond the area which would have served as Duke's living and sleeping quarters. She held up a bag which had been buried underneath some piles of broken branches. It was a sort of small hold-all.

"Do you think it's okay for us to look inside?" she asked.

"I think we should", said James. "I just have this feeling that something is wrong and I'm sure Duke would hardly be hoarding his life savings in there. He's probably hardly got two pennies to rub together, as my granddad would say."

Reluctantly they unzipped the bag and looked inside. All four of them had crowded round the bag, eager to see what might turn up. All four of them froze in horror!

Inside the bag was a black tight-fitting suit with a head-piece, attached to which, was a luminously white face mask!

They all stood in total silence, the gentle breeze rustling the trees and bushes around them. They were stumped and stunned. Duke, their supposed friend and ally in the struggle against the *Men in Black,* was actually one of them. What should they do? What if Duke should come back and find them with the damning piece of evidence against him in their hand? They thought they could hear some movement outside the bushes. They held their breath and stood absolutely still as into the area where they were standing walked the ever-present black cat! *Lucky or unlucky – they weren't sure.*

"What shall we do?" asked Mary, wide eyed with shock.

"We've got to take this piece of evidence with us to the police", said James. "Who knows what it might reveal?"

"All this might be connected to the disappearance of those youngsters off the estate", said Toby.

"I can't believe it!" Harry said. "You just never know, do you?"

"I'm keen to get out of here", said Mary.

They all agreed that they should take the evidence and they crept cautiously out of the bushes, torches switched off, lest they should attract the attention of an irate returning Duke. Once past the end of the lake they began to run – fast. This time the bridge brought no whispered comments about the ghost of Judge Jeffreys. Their minds were fixed on the reality of a man who would not take kindly to the discovery of his dreadful secret. They must put as much distance between them and the park as possible.

The thought of Duke returning perhaps even now, drove them on. They imagined him stooping down to get his gruesome, ghostly outfit. They could see his face red with rage on finding it missing. He would surely know that they were the only ones who would be aware of his hide-away. He would be wild with anger and determined to find them. Perhaps he was the one who had kidnapped the young people along with *Thin Man?* It was becoming clear that his apparent friendliness was a cover to lure them into his confidence. He, along with the other sinister, frightening creatures of the night, was simply waiting an opportunity to drag them into whatever dreadful plans they were scheming. They were weaving a web of deceit into which young people like unsuspecting flies would be drawn and from which it would be difficult, if not impossible, to escape.

As they passed the bridge and began to leave the lake and the park behind them, a pair of eyes watched.

Somehow they sensed it and though out of breath from their earlier exertions they made another dash for the nearby housing estate and the welcome sight of the street lights. Soon they were accelerating down the street that led to Toby's house and safety. Gasping for breath again they bent double in their efforts to try to calm down before entering the house. They were oblivious to the other pair of eyes that noted their exact location and the brief, whispered phone call made by the *Secret Watcher.*

CHAPTER 8

GOT 'IM!

After school on Monday James and Mary called at the police station armed with the evidence – the tight-fitting, black, all-in-one outfit, with the attached, white face mask, found at Duke's place. They had kept it in a plastic carrier, stuffed in Mary's school bag.

They arrived at the station and were shown into Inspector Roberts' office. Bondy's credit with the police was such that he had almost immediate and unquestioned access to the inspector whenever he appeared on the scene with something to offer. His past exploits were now almost part of the folk-lore of the police station!

"Come in Bondy", said the inspector. "Hi Mary; good to see you both" He paused as they sat down and then continued: "Now, what can I do for you? Or, perhaps I should say, what can you do for me?" He grinned broadly as he spoke.

James motioned to Mary and she pulled the black suit out of the plastic carrier and placed it on the table. The inspector leaned back in his chair and whistled through his teeth.

"How do you do it? How *do* you do it? Amazing! So you've caught up with the *Men in Black?"*

"So you know about them?" said James; this time it was his turn to look surprised.

"Yes, James and though I know we are often behind you in our investigations, maybe this time we're just a little bit ahead of you!"

Mary and James looked at one another in puzzlement.

The inspector sat forward in his chair and looked at the two friends. "I take it this is what you found at Duke's hideout?"

"You know him?" said James, struggling to take it all in.

"Yes, indeed we do and we have had our eye on him for some time and were aware of the so called *Men in Black.* However, we have some news for you."

"What's that?" said Mary, as the inspector paused for emphasis.

"We've got him!"

"Got who?" James and Mary chorused together.

"Duke", replied the inspector triumphantly. "And", he went on, "we think we have got the situation sorted. You see we think those *Men in Black* are just meant to be a distraction – a smoke screen, for something bigger. We are questioning Duke and we feel that there is likely to be a very big bank raid in the area. With some persuasion, in terms of lightening his sentence if he cooperates etc, we expect to gain more information and we'll be ready when the time comes. Meantime, the *Men in Black* may well continue their antics, but we will not be distracted by their attempts to scare the public. It seems that Duke was only a 'bit' player and his absence will not be treated with too much suspicion. We will of course keep a minimal police presence around the area so they will still think they've got us hooked."

It was time for James and Mary to fall back into their chairs in astonishment. James was the first to speak:

"Do you know, he had us fooled! We were completely taken in after our initial shock when we bumped into him. He just seemed like the typical loveable rogue, you know, a rough diamond, down on his luck, but really underneath, a good guy."

The inspector smiled once more. "Well, there's more to him than meets the eye, I'm afraid. We know him quite well and as I said, we've been watching him." He paused once again and then said, with a twinkle in his eye: "By the way, what was it that took you down to the park and led to your encounter with Duke?"

Mary was first in with this one: "Oh that was dear young Harry. While out on his midnight prowls he thought he'd seen the ghost of Judge Jeffreys. So we said we'd go and investigate."

"But you haven't met the infamous Judge, I take it?" The inspector was smiling again. Then his smile faded and his jocular tone changed to one of a serious nature. "Look you two, don't take the whole business we've talked about as a joke, will you? I mean these *Men in Black*. Bank robbery is a serious business, so be careful if you go prowling round the park. Tell Harry I said so, wont you?"

They rose to leave, shaking hands with the inspector, who added one more thing as they approached the door.

"Thanks for the *Men in Black* get-up. It could be an important piece of evidence. And keep your eyes peeled and let me know if you see anything suspicious going on.

I have great faith in your powers of detection, Bondy – I mean that seriously. Please keep in touch."

Setting off down the street, they were deep in thought. *What did this latest piece of information mean? So Duke was in on the game with the Men in Black, but where did it fit – if it did – with the Thin Man? Somehow the issue of a bank robbery seemed to put their involvement in a completely different perspective. Lots of jigsaw pieces; but none of them quite fitting together. Who would be involved in the bank robbery? What part could Thin Man play in that? He didn't look like a bank robber. But then, they didn't think Duke could really be involved with the Men in Black. It all seemed crazy and pear-shaped.*

They decided it was time to go home so they went their separate ways; James of course heading for the woods outside the town where he lived with his parents. Mary lived the opposite end of town in the countryside.

Anyway, thought James, I need to concentrate on my course work. I've got a lot of research to do on the ancient Druids and that's going to take a lot of time.

He pedalled on towards the woods; reminding himself that after all, the police were well on with the case. Duke was safely behind bars and with the extra information gleaned from him they would no doubt catch the bank robbers. He wanted to do really well in his A levels as did Mary, so they would have to set aside their detective work and get on with more important things. He had to realise also that they were no longer important players in this game. Leave it to the police.

Bondy did not realise one thing however and that was that he was being followed and had been from the time that they had left the police station. Mary too was being followed, something she did not realise either. As a matter of fact it wouldn't have concerned them, had they known about it. In both cases, they were being followed by policemen, presumably on the inspector's instructions and for their own safety. It seems perhaps the inspector was more aware of things than they realised and it was likely that they were being observed by others too.

In the woods bordering Bondy's home a dark figure lurked and as Mary arrived home she was watched from the shelter of some trees in the field across the way from her house. As the two youngsters entered their homes safely the two policemen pulled up far enough behind them not to be noticed. They spoke for some time on their mobile phones.

Meanwhile the two 'watchers' in the trees also used their mobiles. Their calls were made consecutively with precise timing and only a short message was given. When the first had finished the second call was made. Both *their* calls, however, were answered by a man wearing a black overcoat.

CHAPTER 9

JAMES – I MUST SEE YOU!

Things went quiet, very quiet; maybe too quiet! Bondy & co. made no visits to the park in the evenings. Somehow their enthusiasm was waning, while Harry's midnight wanderings were tailing off too. He was still a bit wary of the ghost of the 'Hanging Judge' as he was called by some. The memory of Duke's description of the mystery *Men in Black* had diminished his enthusiasm. The shock of Duke's own involvement made him wary. There was also the inspector's warning.

Meanwhile Toby was becoming a most diligent student of car mechanics. His visits to the library increased and the number of books he took out could almost have filled a personal library of his own. Of course he insisted – in spite of the redness of his face as he said it – that it was nothing to do with Carol the librarian.

The others teased him about it:

"Come on", said James, "show us some written work you have produced from all this study!"

"It's not like history and that sort of stuff", said Toby defensively. "You don't have to write essays and things; it's completely different. And anyway it's all in my head!"

"But what is it that's in your head?" said Mary, laughing. "That's what I'd like to know. I'll bet it's nothing to do with car mechanics. I bet you don't wake up in the night thinking about cars!"

When Harry was with them he just listened and laughed.

James and Mary were visiting the library on this particular day, when who should they see there, but Toby! Surprise, surprise! And there he was at the car mechanic section listening with rapt attention as Carol, looking as gorgeous as ever; advised him on which book to take out. They tip-toed past and went to the history section, where James in particular, was looking for something a little more detailed on the subject of the Druids.

He wanted, if possible, to get beyond the 'popular' image of the bloodthirsty, human and even child-sacrificing Druid, which went back to Roman times and the ancient Britons – the original Welsh people.

When Carol had finished with Toby – who still followed her around like a little puppy dog – she came over to James and Mary, giving them a big wink. Which being interpreted meant, *don't worry about Toby, I can handle him and he's a really nice lad!* They both grinned back at her, James calling out in as casual a way as possible:

"Hey there Toby, got some more books to study?"

Toby shook his fist at him behind Carol's back, knowing exactly what he was getting at, but still grinning from ear to ear!

James was keen to ask Carol a question – not about books on the Druids, but rather on the likely sightings of the *Thin Man.*

"No", she replied. "Thank goodness I've not seen anything of him since that last time when you were here."

"Let's hope we don't see any more of him either", said Mary. "He gives me the creeps!"

"And we're all agreed on that", said Toby managing to tear his gaze away from the delectable Carol.

"Have you seen anything of our old history teacher, Granville Davies – Granny, as we used to affectionately call him?"

"Yes", replied Carol. "He's been in quite a few times, but not in the main library. He's been in the ancient manuscript section looking up something, I suppose for the Historical Society. They had a meeting recently and no doubt something has come up on which he wants to do some research."

James looked knowingly at Mary and then Toby, but he made no further comment, just nodding his head.

After a few more exchanges of pleasantries one to the other, they left the library. In one hand James was clutching a new book on the Druids. With the other he was managing to drag Toby out through the door as he cast longing looks behind him, to where the glamorous librarian stood giving them a little wave as they departed.

"I hope you're going to get stuck into that book on car maintenance, or whatever it is", said James grinning and just managing to leap onto his bike before Toby grabbed him. "See you later", he shouted as they all sped off to their separate homes. He could see Toby grinning but shaking his fist threateningly as he rounded the corner and was lost from view.

That evening James was planning a session of study, especially of the new book he had found on the Druids. However when he got home, his mother greeted him with the news that a letter had arrived, marked urgent. Puzzled, he opened it at once to find a hastily scribbled note from his old friend and former teacher – Granny:

James

I must see you at once. I have made a discovery which I think you will find very interesting. Moreover, I feel this is urgent, so could you come here tonight at 8 p m?

Yours,
Granville Davies

James sat down in his room and thought deeply:

What could it be about? Had Granny found the old manuscript, or the missing part? Why was it so urgent? He felt somehow that the tone of the note gave the impression that Granny was holding back his deepest feelings about the new-found information, whilst underneath, he was desperate to see James.

It had to be tonight, so after tea, and an hour or so on the ancient Druids, Bondy set off on his bike for Granny's house. His heart was beating fast. He had a tense, insistent feeling inside him that he was on the brink of something really big. What it was he could not begin to guess. He began to pedal faster, the words 'this is urgent' racing through his brain. How urgent? Was there some kind of danger? He rounded the corner and sped into the street where Granny lived. He pulled up at the kerb, propped his bike up against the kerb, and climbed up the few steps that led to the front door. The church bell struck eight! He was bang on time. That must be why Granny had left the front door ajar. *He would know that I was usually on time for lessons, so he left it for me to go straight in.*

He knocked first, out of politeness and waited to hear the familiar voice of his former history teacher calling out: 'Come on in lad and sit yourself down'. He had a smile on his face as he recalled the fond greeting of his favourite teacher.

But the smile turned to an expression of puzzlement as he pushed open the door slightly. Then it became one of extreme alarm as he entered a room that looked as though a bomb had hit it! Chairs were turned over and in some cases the fabric of the chairs had been ripped open, pieces of torn fabric lying strewn across the floor. Books lay scattered around the room, some of them torn and stripped of their hard covers. Almost every piece of furniture had been tipped over, drawers pulled out and their contents spilled out across the floor.

Bondy felt like crying. He knew how precious some of those books would have been to Granny. But then it hit him like a blow to the stomach! Where was he? Where was Granny? What had happened to him? Perhaps he was upstairs? He called out, softly at first and then more loudly:

"Mr Davies, are you there sir? It's James here, are you all right?"

He heard a sound upstairs and breathed a sigh of relief. In spite of this mess, he was ok he was upstairs, thank God! Then he heard footsteps charging down the stairs at amazing speed. That was never Granny! He waited, wondering who it could be, yet holding himself ready, just in case.

The footsteps drew nearer and then round the corner of the winding stair came a familiar figure. He was wearing a black overcoat! James wasted no time; he shot out of the doorway, stumbled down the steps, and fell headlong into his bike. He picked it up and leapt upon it, his foot coming down on the pedal and moving the bike forward almost in one swift movement. He sped off down the road, not daring to glance back until he had put some distance between himself and the dreaded *Thin Man.* What had happened to Granny and why? Where was he? And where was all this leading?

PART TWO

THE SECRET CODE

"The Shadow cloaked from head to foot"

Tennyson

The four captive teenagers were frightened. They were not usually frightened – not so you'd notice anyway. But now they *were* frightened! That day they had been led down a dark tunnel – it seemed to go on for ages, with only the dim light of a torch to guide them. The man in the lead was not a nice man. He was mean, very mean. As teenagers messing around on the edges of gang battles which occasionally resulted in violence they had thought of themselves as mean and hard. But this was different and they did not like it! They had no control and no real knowledge of where it would end.

The food and the drinks had disappeared and the grand promises had been daily and hourly fading into the mist like a dream from which one awakes with a start to face reality. Somehow all the bravado and the bluster had gone and the fight was being knocked out of them. The softening up process had worked well for *Thin Man* and his cronies. They were trapped and disorientated – there was nowhere to go. They had been lured into the spider's web like silly flies and there was no way out.

They were in a dark tunnel in more senses than one, but the tunnel down which they were making their way from the grand mansion in which they had been housed for some weeks, was real enough. *Where were they going? They did not know. Why were they going there? Again, they did not know. They were in the dark and the darkness was as black as the thick darkness of the tunnel along which they were now dragging their weary feet. The weariness was not due to physical tiredness or hunger - they had lived in luxury up to this point. No; it was the uncertainty and the crippling sense of fear of the unknown that gripped them, draining the strength from their legs.*

They reached the end of the tunnel; at least they assumed it was the end because they found themselves walking into a much wider area. It was a sort of large room, damp and smelly as if no one had been in it for years. In a totally unceremonious way they were handed spades and told to dig in a certain spot.

"If you do well you'll be rewarded", said the man, with an evil grin on his face. He paused and then he grinned again, continuing; "But don't get slack or lazy, or it could go badly for you!"

As he said this, he smacked the solid looking stick he was carrying, into the palm of his huge hand. They wanted to protest, or perhaps rush him and try to overpower him – but it was useless. He was huge, like some kind of all-in wrestler. They picked up their spades and began to dig .....

CHAPTER 1

GRANNY IS MISSING!

James arrived home breathless. His parents were watching something on the television. Should he tell them? It was difficult to know which course of action was best. So far he had said nothing to them of his most recent adventures and his visit to his former history teacher was not unusual. He was seventeen now and his parents were sensitive to his growing adulthood and respected his need to do his own thing and make his own decisions. Their relationship was good and they always shared problems and things they had in common. But there were things that were kept to themselves, as should be the case in a good relationship where there is mutual trust.

He decided to say nothing unless pressed to do so by circumstances. He popped his head round the door to tell them he was off to bed and to say 'goodnight'. However, once upstairs James 'Bondy' Evans did do something he regularly did – he prayed. Being a Christian it was natural for him to do so – a bit like breathing really! It was of course something he shared with Mary and increasingly also with Toby, Harry and others. His fellow pupils at school had come to respect him and also his faith, though there were still many who sneered at the whole idea of God and prayer – at least on the surface they did. Their view was that in this scientific age it was rather ridiculous, to say the least, to be praying and believing in God. James knew of many scientists – some famous ones – who were Christians, so he didn't see how the issue could be about science. And as far as prayer was concerned he remembered being told that Einstein once urged a student looking for something to research, that he should consider researching the mystery of prayer! Einstein was hardly a simple minded person who didn't use his brain, was he?

After praying, he thought deeply about what had happened. He wondered why Granny had sent for him. *Had he discovered something? If he had, why hadn't he told him in the letter? Perhaps it was too sensitive to put in a letter that might fall into the wrong hands? Perhaps it was better discussed face to face?* He looked again at the letter in case there was anything in it that was a clue to what it was all about. He wondered if there was something in the house that Granny had intended to give him. It was obvious that *Thin Man* had been searching for something, unless of course, he just happened to call and find the place in a mess and was upstairs looking for Granny. *Mmmm doubtful!* The question was; where was Granny? Perhaps he *was* upstairs? James was extremely doubtful about that and if he wasn't; where was he?

James knew he would have to go to the house, first of all to make sure Granny was no longer there and secondly to see whether he could find any clues as to Granny's purpose in sending the urgent letter. He had responded earlier to a call of 'Goodnight' from his parents and he could tell by the noises he had heard a while ago and also by the silence that had descended upon the house; that his parents had retired to their bedroom. He could not leave it for another twenty four hours before he went to investigate. He had to go now!

He changed into some older clothes because he intended going through the woods and across the fields on foot. He would be less likely to be seen and also this would lead him to the back entrance of the house, where he hoped he would find some means of entry. Someone could be watching the front.

It was now completely dark and the moon was hidden behind the clouds. He took a torch and set off, creeping silently down the stairs, out through the back door and into the woods bordering their cottage. He began a steady running pace similar to that often employed by him in his record breaking four hundred metre races. Before long he had left the woods behind and was racing across the fields beyond which Granny's house lay. The houses adjoining Granny's home were in complete darkness so he approached the back garden gate at a run and vaulted easily and noiselessly over it. In no time he was outside the back window of the house.

Granny had always been a stickler for fresh air:

"Boy at the back, open the window, will you? I can hardly breathe in here!"

True to form, the window had been left just slightly open to let some air in, no doubt to dispel the smells from the kitchen. It was easy to open it and squeeze through the gap. He dropped down silently onto the kitchen floor, holding his breath just in case the slightest sound had alerted someone in the house. Not Granny, of course! He was convinced that he had been kidnapped, but he had no idea whether anybody had been left behind to keep an eye on the place. He crept towards the living room and entered, stubbing his toe against an upturned chair. He winced slightly and then as he reached the window, looked outside to see if there was anyone loitering suspiciously and perhaps watching the house. *No one!*

He switched his torch on and swept the beam around the room. The place was exactly as he had seen it before his hasty departure. There were books everywhere, torn pages and sheets of paper. He knelt down and examined by the torch-light the papers and the pages from the books and anything else that could possibly have contained any note or hidden message that would help him. *No luck!* He was about to go upstairs when he heard a banging noise up above the staircase. He froze on the spot! *Someone was up there!* Slowly he crept up the stairs, pausing at each step to avoid any creaks. Reaching the top, he paused again, holding his breath and peering round the first bedroom door - *that bang again!* But to his relief, he saw the open bedroom window swinging outwards in the gentle, night-time breeze. He checked the other bedrooms and the bathroom.

There had clearly been some disturbance up in the bedrooms, but nothing like the chaos downstairs. He decided to return to the living room. At least he had satisfied himself that Granny was not in the house. He shook his head, feeling rather frustrated. Was there anything there for him? He knelt down once more on the floor and shone his torch round the room. *Then he saw it!* Underneath the one piece of furniture that remained standing he spied a piece of paper. Was it an envelope? He scrambled across and lying down on his stomach managed to reach it and pull it out. It was an envelope and it had written on it: *Bondy's project.*

He grinned to himself and his heart began to beat a little faster. *Perhaps they had never seen this in their mad search and devastation of the room. Or maybe they had seen it and considered it of no importance. They would surely not know who Bondy was! Moreover he had the feeling that if this proved significant, which it surely would, it would reveal how crafty Granny was. After all he rarely called James 'Bondy' and anyway James was not doing a project with Granny – except perhaps, the one that involved Thin Man's search for the manuscript!*

He tore back the overlap of the envelope, his fingers trembling and this is what he read:

Well, Bondy, these are my comments on your latest piece of work. Perhaps I am going to 'dictote some nates' to you as in days gone by!

But do take my comments seriously won't you, in spite of my little joke!

I have graded your work according to a new system of grading which you ought to remember from our conversation previously.

1) 4 K9 – this is the first part; and you've made a good start here for your study.

2)4 x C. This is the second part. Rather long and rushed. You're not running in your favourite race you know!

I think you should go to the library and do some more research. I'm afraid you're going to have to dig deeper if you're to win the history prize.

Anyway, I wish you well.

G Davies

Bondy gazed at the note in astonishment. It was nonsense, surely? What was he on about? Was there some hidden message? Was there some sort of secret code? He'd have to do some more praying and some more deep thinking!

Just then, he was convinced he heard a noise. It sounded like a door being opened very quietly. He held his breath, turning his head in the direction of the door. He could see the handle moving ever so slightly. He got to his feet, hastily stuffing the vital message into his belt bag. He must not lose it! It had to be saying something.

The door was now opening and a hand appeared on the side of the door. No time for delay! He shot towards the opposite door leading to the kitchen and the back entrance. A quick glance over his shoulder revealed a white face mask peering round the door. It was one of those weird freaks they had seen in the park. It looked like a disembodied face on account of the totally black covering below.

James shot through the door, into the kitchen. He literally leapt onto the sink unit below the kitchen window, grabbed at the window, twisting the handle and pushing it open in one movement. A strong hand grasped his trailing leg as he attempted to dive out of the window onto the lawn below. Instinctively he kicked out fiercely with his other leg and felt a solid impact at the end of his foot. There was a muffled cry of pain and his leg broke free.

So far so good, but now he was dropping head first towards the ground. His excellent athleticism came in handy as he managed to roll into a ball and land without too much discomfort on the lawn below. Leaping to his feet, he shot like lightning towards the back gate, and hurdling it like an Olympic runner, headed across the field. James could run. He held the record for under eighteens in

Wales at four hundred metres. But a swift look behind told him that the figure in pursuit was no slouch at running either.

These men – if men they were – clearly meant business and James could feel the fear rising from the pit of his stomach. The fear increased when in the distance from two sides, a group of similarly clad ghostly figures emerged, racing to cut him off. He must gain the woods! There were six of them and they were forming a kind of scissor movement across the field. He had to make it. He dreaded to think what would happen if he didn't.

He fixed his eyes upon the line of trees that formed the entrance to the forest a few hundred yards away and he ran! Strange and fiendish cries echoed in the night air as the hunters with the white faces closed in on their prey. The figure behind him was falling behind, but the gap ahead was narrowing – it was touch and go! If they closed it he was done for!

Gritting his teeth, James surged forward and as the last fifty metres or so arrived, he put in that final burst for which he was renowned in his numerous competitions. As if in overdrive, he suddenly rocketed through the ever narrowing gap and disappeared into the forest.

Disappeared was evidently the right word. The ghostly figures hurled themselves into the dark woods, but could see no sign of him. Everything was still. They were baffled. Where was he? They could hear no sound of someone crashing through trees or undergrowth far ahead. They began to search, spreading out almost in military style. He had disappeared so quickly – he must be hiding, but where?

James could see them and hear them. At one point they were almost in touching distance. His heart was in his mouth. He could scarcely breathe. They were parting the bushes and probing around in the undergrowth.

Please God! The Lord is our refuge and strength, a very present help in trouble. They were so close, so very close. They moved away, but then one of them came back. James could hear him cursing under his breath. *So maybe they were human after all!*

And yet James could almost smell the evil from so close a distance. He was hanging on by his fingers to a jagged piece of rock. The rock was now cutting into his skin. His grip was slipping. He was in what was left of the entrance to an old mine shaft. It was hidden by the thick bushes to all but those who had discovered it. As far as he knew, James was the only one who had. It was only entered by the smallest of gaps. He had squeezed through it in his panic to escape, scraping his knees and elbows and wincing in pain. If he slipped, he would slide inexorably down the slope and into the awesome depths of the mine shaft itself. He would never normally have entered it, but he had no choice. In that split second, that critical nick of time that many often face, he had to decide and act.

He was now wondering whether he should have surrendered. Yet in his heart he knew he never could.

After half an hour they gave up amid more cursing and muttering. Still he waited another five minutes, convinced that he had heard their departing footsteps clearly enough to be sure they had really gone. Slowly, painfully, he crawled out through the narrow gap, pausing on the edge, once his legs were clear of the dreadful drop over which he had been suspended. He lay there for some time gathering his senses, breathing deeply. He muttered a prayer of thanks.

He could not relax. They might still be around. Making his way slowly, he strained his ears for any tell-tale sounds of activity or movement up ahead. He kept to the hidden areas of the woods known so well to him, avoiding the obvious paths. Exhausted, he eventually reached his cottage on the far edge of the woods. Still he waited, before walking up the path to the welcome sanctuary of his home.

CHAPTER 2

CRACKING THE CODE

That night as he lay in bed James was deep in thought. Granny was missing and it must be reported to the police. He lived alone and it was unlikely that anyone had yet noticed his absence. But on the other hand, if he told the police and it became general knowledge, it might make things more dangerous as far as Granny himself was concerned. There was no doubt now that he was being held by utterly ruthless men and that *Thin Man* and the 'ghost squad' who had just terrorised him in the frantic chase across the field were working hand in hand.

It might be better if he gave them the impression that they had scared him off. If he was honest they almost had! He was still trembling at the thought, so vivid in his young mind, of that pack of hungry, savage wolves which almost sank their teeth into him. Had they caught him.... he shivered at the thought of what they might have done.

If he could work out what this mysterious message was about and then take things from there, then perhaps he could see the problem more clearly. It was a difficult decision, but he decided, reluctantly, to say nothing to the police.

After school that evening he and Mary and Toby got together to discuss the mysterious letter left by Granny. There was a stunned silence when he related his story of the narrow escape and the chase across the fields. He showed them the cuts on his hands and arms when he had clung for life on the precipitous edge of the hidden mine shaft. The other two stood open-mouthed and shocked, unable to speak at first. Then they both huddled around Bondy holding him close – Mary in tears, Toby with a grim look of both deep concern and anger on his face.

They felt utterly sick at the thought of what had happened to James, and of dear old Granny being hurt in any way. But when they had calmed down, they were all agreed that it was within their power to help him if only they could understand the contents of the letter.

They met at Toby's where they spread the letter out on the kitchen table. First they prayed together; then they discussed the contents of the mysterious message – the *Secret Code.*

"What on earth does it mean?" said Toby gazing at the letter with a frown on his face.

"It's beyond me", said Mary, "but if we go through it phrase by phrase, maybe something will come."

They all agreed that the "latest piece of work" had to refer to their visit to Granny and their question about the *Thin Man* and the possible existence of another manuscript or a missing piece of the manuscript. Granny said that perhaps he was going to *dictote some nates* as he so amusingly put it. He was clearly aware that they used to tease him about his mixing up of his vowels and his words. They decided that he had put that in deliberately to warn them that what he was about to write, was not quite as it seemed.

But what about this new system of grading – they'd never come across any such system, new or old!

"Exactly", said Mary, "because what he is telling us, or rather you Bondy, is not about a grade for your work at all. For a start you're not actually doing any work in history for him. He's just hoping that if this letter had been looked at by "Mr Black Overcoat" he would have assumed it was some sort of system of grading. But it's not; it contains some sort of secret coded message to you."

"I'm sure you're right Mary, but what does it mean?" James was nodding and looking puzzled at the same time.

"Then there's this first part", said Toby, warming to the task and placing a can of coke in front of each of them as he spoke. "It says 4 K9 – what could that be about?" He scratched his head and then his eyes lit up and a broad grin split his face.

"Hey, wasn't there a dog in a film – like a robot – and they called it K9, you know, like another way of saying 'canine', which is the proper term for a dog. But it can't be that, of course - just a guess on my part."

"But that's what we've got to do", said James. "You know, think outside the box; be imaginative."

"Okay, so 4 K9 could perhaps be 'four dogs'", said Mary.

"What if he's not referring to real dogs, but to the 'Four Dogs' at the old entrance of the driveway to where the old hall used to be?" James was leaning forward eagerly and looking excitedly at the other two.

"And it goes on to say that it makes 'a good start for your study' which could mean that we have to start there in order to find something", said Mary sipping her coke excitedly.

"I think we went to see them for part of a history lesson", said James. "You know, the dogs, like statues on top of the four pillars at the big gateway. Everybody knows the Four Dogs, but I think they were put there by Sir *somebody or other* in 1820. He was the owner at the time. I've forgotten his name. And don't forget, the *Thin Man* went to see Granny and was asking about a manuscript to do with the old hall – you know, where Judge Jeffreys used to live."

"What about this next bit, then," said Toby, tipping his head back as he downed the last drops of his coke.

They looked at the words 4 x C and noticed that the 'x' was a small one, not like the other letters, so perhaps it meant 'times', as in '4 times' something in multiplication. But what about the 'C'? It looked like an average sort of grade, but what if it was a Roman numeral – didn't that stand for 100?

"It says it's long and rushed, so we should take our time. Maybe it means 400 years, something that's very old. Or maybe it means a distance of 400 metres?" Toby was getting excited now!

"That's it!" James punched the air in triumph. "Well done Toby! Look he mentions my favourite race which is the 400 metres - how clever!"

"In other words", said Mary, "we start at the Four Dogs and 400 metres from there we have to look for something. And, wait a minute, 'go to the library and do some more research', what does that mean?"

They were silent for a while and then James broke in again:

"How about this: we go to the library and maybe Carol has been given something by Granny. He knows she always helps us with research. Maybe what she gives us – if she does – will help us further. The digging deeper bit could be meant literally – we've got to dig somewhere."

They looked at each other with a mixture of excitement and puzzlement. They could just be guessing and yet, it had to be something like that.

"We'll go to the library tomorrow after school", said James. Then he paused and looked thoughtful and a little troubled.

"There's one thing that's bothering me. *Thin Man* saw me at Granny's house and I have no doubt he'll be watching me. Last night was proof of just what he and they are capable of. That's one reason why I'm glad I've not been to the police. If he thought I was doing that it could put Granny in greater danger. If he thinks I've been scared off, maybe it will give us that bit more time to find Granny. I must try to stay low for a while."

"What if I was to go into the library and see if Carol has a message for you?" said Toby, smiling broadly.

"Actually, that could be a good idea", said James, grinning at the speed with which Toby offered his services! "After all no one would see anything unusual in you visiting Carol!"

Toby leaned across and gave James a playful punch on the arm. James laughed but then became serious:

"I really do mean it, Tobe; it would be a great way of getting the message – if there is one – without arousing suspicion."

All three of them agreed, but then their thoughts turned to the plight of Granny. *If only they knew where he was!*

Granny was in fact sitting in a rather comfortable armchair, drinking a glass of very good quality wine. He was in the company of his fellow historian – he of the black overcoat. They had been chatting about things historical and swapping tales of ancient discoveries and old manuscripts. *Thin Man* had apologised profusely for the rough handling of the previous night and had assured Granny that those kinds of methods were not really to his liking. Sadly it had been necessary at the time, but he was sure that they could come to an amicable agreement in due course.

Granny smiled a broad, but totally unbelieving smile and sipped his wine. "I like the wine", he said, "crisp and refreshing with a suggestion of fruity flavours."

At that point the phone rang and it was answered promptly by his host.

"Yes, he's here, just sharing a glass of wine with me. Yes, as you say, that is imperative. Don't worry about it. Any news on the progress with the boys? I hope they are cooperating. Good, excellent. Hopefully that will not be necessary. I'll keep you informed."

He put the phone down and looked across at Granny, who by now having drained his glass, was considering filling up again, but thought better of it and replaced the glass on the table.

"I hope you find your accommodation acceptable?" his host said smiling thinly once more. "We do aim to please, Mr Davies and as students of the same scholarly discipline, it is my hope that our relationship can be to our mutual benefit."

"I'm sure I would love to be helpful to you in any way I can, provided you can fully explain to me what exactly is the purpose of your 'cloak and dagger' enterprise." Granny met his gaze and smiled pleasantly.

"Come now, Mr Davies, 'cloak and dagger' as you call it, is a rather harsh way of describing an enterprise arising out of scholarly concern and prolonged study of ancient documents." He smiled thinly once again, shaking his head in mock disbelief.

Granny's reply was instant: "I'm sorry if I sound harsh, but your explanation of your treatment of me last night does not satisfy me, nor does it fit with my conception of scholarly research." This time the smile faded from Granny's face and in its place was a steely look of unwavering determination.

"I am so sorry to hear that, my friend", was the reply. "However I must warn you it may become necessary to use a little more persuasion if you persist in being stubborn. Meanwhile, I will bid you goodnight and hope that you sleep well."

He rose promptly and left the room, his face red with fury and frustration. The large clock on the wall chimed midnight!

CHAPTER 3

TOBY MEETS THE THIN MAN

The next day, after his college course for the morning was over, Toby set off for the library. In spite of James's and Mary's assurances that he would not be under suspicion, he kept his eyes peeled in case he *was* being followed. He went on foot, thinking it would make it more difficult for him to be followed – he didn't notice anything suspicious.

Arriving at the library, he made his way immediately – as was his custom – to the desk where the delectable Carol usually sat. To his surprise, she was not there. Instead a rather plain-looking, sharp-featured, older woman was manning the enquiry desk. Toby could not hide his disappointment and she could not veil the suspicious look that clouded her face as she looked up at him.

"How may I help you?" she said without a trace of a smile.

"Oh…er; my name is Toby and I was expecting to see Carol."

"I take it you mean Mrs Parry?" she said, interrupting him and giving him a disapproving look at his use of the first name.

"Well, you see, she always gives me advice regarding my car mechanics books and I thought…."

Once again she interrupted him with an even fiercer look of disapproval.

"Does she indeed? Well, I'm afraid she's not here today, having taken the day off through sickness. However, young man, she did leave a book for you on car mechanics, in case you called."

She paused as Toby's face broke into a smile and then continued:

"Personally, mind you, I am not so sure that chasing around for books for you young people is exactly the best use of her time. Here is your book." She handed it to him without smiling.

Toby took the book and turned to leave, thanking the lady for being helpful and clutching his prize to his chest, noting as he did so that it smelt of Carol's favourite perfume!

Something made him pause as he was about to leave the building and instead he turned into a side room to have a look at the latest book from his favourite librarian. As he sat down at one of the tables, he caught a glimpse of his least favourite library visitor – there was a flash of a long black overcoat passing the doorway! He had just opened the book and it was lying on the desk in front of him. His eyes strayed back down to the page as he tried to keep one eye open to see where the 'black overcoat' was going. He was out of sight, talking angrily to the substitute librarian.

He gasped as he looked down, for there fastened to the inner page, were two notes in sealed envelopes.

One addressed to 'Toby', in what was obviously Carol's handwriting and the other addressed to 'Bondy', in Granny's handwriting. His heart was pounding. He quickly tore open the note addressed to him and read it, whilst doing his best to keep an eye open for his arch enemy.

Toby,

I hope you get this note and the one for James. Mr Davies was so anxious that it was passed on to him. The man in the black overcoat has been around more than ever just lately and I am now quite fearful of his intentions. He seems to see me as some sort of go-between, collecting and passing on information and his manner has been increasingly threatening. My husband is away on business at the moment and I am troubled about this whole affair.

Keep an eye out for me won't you?
Carol x

At that moment Toby saw *Thin Man* passing the doorway and he quickly buried his head in his book till he felt the coast was clear. Once he was as sure as he could be, he leapt to his feet and ran to the door. He was just in time to see the black saloon car making its way slowly, in heavy traffic down the main street. He now began to curse his luck that he didn't have his bike with him. At least he could have followed them for a while and maybe found out where they were going.

Just then a battered old banger-of-a-car came round the corner. It was Alfie from the estate, in his pride and joy – an old Ford Mondeo. He was a bit of a self-taught car mechanic, was Alfie. He'd tinkered around with this one and it sounded and performed like a racing car. Toby waved him down frantically and the car screeched to a halt with a rattle and a bang.

There was no time for any fancy introductions. Alfie knew Toby well and was one of his most ardent boxing fans - Toby being the 'Under Eighteen Champion of Wales.'

"Alfie", shouted Toby, "follow that car – the black one."

"No problem, champ," replied Alfie with a smile; "it's no contest!"

With a grating of gears and a mighty roar reminiscent of the Grand Prix races, they shot off in pursuit of the still visible black saloon. Alfie was clearly enjoying himself and so was Toby – up to a point! The black saloon had got a good start and Alfie's efforts to catch up left Toby hanging on for dear life as they tore round an 'S' bend on the country lane, just missing a lone cyclist. Toby spotted him through the rear window, wobbling and then finally crashing into a ditch! He breathed a prayer of thanks as he just caught sight of him rising up from the ditch, before he was lost to sight round the next bend.

"Ease up Alfie", said Toby, "and keep a reasonable distance. I don't want them to know they're being followed!"

There had just been an almighty screeching of brakes as they barely kept on four wheels at the next bend.

"Hey, sorry Tobe, I thought they was friends of yours and you were off to a party somewhere!" Alfie was grinning from ear to ear as he spoke.

"No chance of a party where we are heading", said Toby grimly.

The car ahead was easing up and indicating a right turn into a huge driveway. They watched as it turned up the drive and then stopped.

"Drive past and pull up a little way ahead", said Toby. Alfie did so.

They sat in the car for a while and then Toby asked Alfie to stay in the car while he went to have a look. He crept along the hedgerow, keeping out of sight of the drive area. Looking round the corner and up the drive he could see that the car appeared to be empty. Where had they gone? He went up to the car, looking towards his right where he could see a rather grand looking summer house. They must have gone there for some reason. He reached the car, crouching down out of view of the summer house. To his amazement the car door against which he was crouching had a familiar smell. He could smell Carol's perfume and no, it was not just from his shirt where he had held the library book. It was definitely from the car door. *Carol had been in this car at some time! Was she in that summer house? Toby would have bet on it! Somehow it didn't seem likely she had only just been brought there. Perhaps she was under guard there and the other two men were calling to check on things? Could be.*

Quickly, he crept stealthily down the drive and then ran back to Alfie. He asked him if he would do him another favour, after explaining briefly the real nature of the chase. He wanted him to listen carefully and if Toby whistled to come running to the summer house prepared for action!

"Anything you say Tobe", was his reply, with a knowing wink and a nod.

Toby ran back to the edge of the drive, pulling up just in time to see the *Thin Man* and another man getting back into the car. He was still convinced that there was someone in the summer house. He was betting that Carol was there with another person – possibly a guard of some kind.

He watched the car as it disappeared round the bend at the top of the drive and finally out of sight. He sped across the grass to the summer house and crept up to the window. Inching his way up he managed to get himself in a position to peer round the corner of the window and into the small room. There seated on a chair, bound and gagged was his delectable Carol. His blood boiled as he saw her desperate plight. He was about to rush in, when he caught sight of the other occupant of the room. He was a huge brute-of-a-man, well over six feet tall and built like an all-in wrestler. He was standing in the corner, leering at Carol, cracking his knuckles and flexing his massive muscles. Toby thought to himself – *He probably has iron bars for a snack, not chocolate bars. And somehow I've got to get past him!*

CHAPTER 4

THE BIGGER THEY ARE....

'The harder they fall' – well, that was the theory! Toby was weighing up his chances in a desperate plan to rescue Carol. He recalled some of his boxing matches.

Why, only a few weeks ago, I was up against an opponent almost as big as this guy. I kept out of his way, waited my chance and caught him with a beauty. Down he went and out for the count! So, maybe I stand a chance. On the other hand, in the small confines of this summer house...difficult. If he gets hold of me he could probably break me in two.

Then he smelt Carol's perfume on his shirt, where the library book had been held, close to his heart! And that settled it – he was going in! He thought quickly of some way of approaching the 'man mountain' that might give him some advantage. Nothing really came to him, nothing at all. He braced himself and simply charged into the summer house, prepared for anything. To his amazement, as he burst into the room, he saw that the guard, in those few moments while Toby was thinking what to do, had picked up a comic from the book-case against the wall.

He was now sitting in the chair to Toby's left, engrossed in his reading matter, with a big grin on his face. He was reading the latest adventure of 'Dennis the Menace', his face screwed up in concentration.

He began rising shakily to his feet as the door swung open. This was definitely *not* 'Dennis the Menace'; this was Toby the Terror, his face ablaze with a kind of righteous anger! The guard never quite made it to his feet. Toby leapt forward, light on *his* feet as in the boxing ring, planting his right foot forward to give maximum power to his favoured left to the body. Then with all the strength he could muster, and with all the pent up anger at what had been done to Carol, he hit him full on in the stomach.

The man was indeed huge and muscular, generally speaking. The one place, in particular where he was rather flabby on account of his excessive drinking, was his stomach. Toby felt his fist sink into the flab and watched the brute gasp in agony, doubling up breathlessly, falling towards the floor. But light as a dancer on his feet, and before the man reached the floor, Toby, moving with the downward momentum of the man's body, shoved him with all his considerable strength towards the summer house wall. It was made of rather thin woodwork and it had never been asked in the past to withstand the power of seventeen stones or more of body weight crashing against it. It was unable to deal with it and duly smashed, splintered and broke, leaving the guard helpless and thoroughly dazed, with his head, shoulders and arms, protruding out of the wall. He looked a fine specimen of which many a hunter would have been proud!

Toby wasted no time admiring his efficient piece of demolition. Sticking his head out of the door, he gave Alfie the promised whistle and then immediately turned his attention to Carol. She was gazing mutely at him with astonishment and admiration, her eyes shining her appreciation at his bravery and mastery of the brutal guard. He swiftly removed the gag from her mouth and with his pen knife began cutting through the ropes that bound her hands and feet. Just then, Alfie arrived, stopping briefly to whistle through his teeth at the prize specimen hanging on the summer house wall. The man was coming round slowly, but the sight of Alfie standing in front of him wielding a huge spanner, killed any thoughts of possible attempts to escape.

In spite of the seriousness of the situation Alfie could not help releasing another admiring, though utterly respectful whistle, as the lovely Carol emerged through the door holding Toby's hand.

"Let's go, Alf", said Toby, "and this time don't spare the horses!"

They ran across the field, down the drive and climbing into Alfie's car, they sped off down the road with a roar and a squeal of tyres.

"Head for Mary's", said Toby, "I'll direct you. She'll be safe there."

Mary's parents, he knew, were away on business. Her father, the owner of a large computer business had taken his wife with him. By this time, Mary would be home, as a quick call on his mobile confirmed, while another call to Bondy ensured that he too would be on his way as soon as possible. No one was following and they arrived without any mishap.

That evening they all sat in the spacious lounge reflecting on the day's events - apart from Alfie, who had returned home with Toby's grateful words of appreciation ringing in his ears. There was much to think about and to take in and, of course, there was the mysterious note sent to Bondy via Carol and then Toby, They couldn't wait to open it, but they did wait, until Carol had told them her story and Toby had related his daring and successful rescue attempt.

Carol, it seemed, after the earlier mentioned threats, suspected that she was being followed. And on the previous evening, before Toby's visit to the library, two men had called at her home – her husband being away of course, on business. *Thin Man* was one of the visitors and he was accompanied by the driver of the black car. On the pretext that he required some help with his research, he managed to persuade Carol to allow them in. Once in, however, the mood changed. Clearly, they were suspicious of her involvement with Granny and Bondy, reckoning that she knew something or was acting as a go-between in the affair. They took her that night and in the morning rang the library to inform them, on her behalf, that she was sick.

Next, they all listened with a mixture of astonishment and amusement as Toby related his story. Carol leapt in to describe the scene of the final 'showdown' in the summer house.

"You would not believe it, James and Mary, honestly, he was amazing and so brave..."

At this point tears came into her eyes as she remembered the fear that had gripped her during those long hours of captivity and the relief beyond possible measure, when the door had burst open and her *Superman* had hurtled into the room.

"He was magnificent and I don't know how he did it", she said, still wiping the tears from her eyes.

"That brute was just flattened and smashed through the wall. You can't believe what he did. He's a hero and I really don't know what I can give him as a reward for his courage and marvellous strength."

"I know what you can give me", said Toby, with just about the biggest grin ever seen on his cheerful, open face. "That lovely letter you sent me had a kiss at the bottom. All I ask is to claim that kiss." He was wiping tears from his own eyes as he spoke.

Carol leapt to her feet, the tears flowing again down her face, threw her arms around Toby and kissed him on both cheeks and finally gently on his lips. Then she sat down beside him on the sofa with her arms around him, smiling happily. Toby was speechless and simply said nothing, struggling to deal with his own emotions.

Bondy and Mary looked on with huge smiles on their faces. James spoke out:

"Toby is what you might call a gentle giant and also a giant gentleman. He's helped both of us out of a few scrapes, I can tell you. And from what you've said Tobe, I reckon we've now got a pretty good idea as to where our dear old friend Granny is. What you've done is fantastic!"

"But there's one more thing, Bondy", said Mary, putting her arm round him. "What about your note from Granny? You've not looked at it yet."

James reached into his pocket and pulled out the note. He opened it and as he did so the room went quiet. Somehow everybody in that room knew that the contents of the envelope could provide a vital key to the whole mystery. He read out what was written inside, in a loud clear voice, while the eyes of all of them were fixed intently on his face, taking in every word he uttered. They could hear the clock on the wall ticking and their own hearts beating to its steady relentless rhythm.

CHAPTER 5

A RHYME AND A RIDDLE?

The letter was rather lengthy and bore all the hallmarks of having been written in great haste.

Dear James

I am writing this to you in the hope that it may help you in your quest to outdo the ruthless men who are clearly intent on something quite abominable. A member of my history society came across this lost piece of the manuscript quite by chance – though knowing your Christian beliefs, I'm sure you will dispute the chance element. He was not even aware that he had it and almost threw it away!

I am sure you will have solved the mystery of my secret code – if you are reading this you must have understood it to some extent because you will have gone to the library and 'done some research'. At the time I was forced to separate the two pieces of information and use the code in case it fell into their hands.

Yes, you must start at the Four Dogs entrance just off the main road and measure 400 metres along the drive, towards the site of the old hall. At that point you will need to dig down – don't know how far, I'm afraid. I am simply giving the information from the manuscript which I had seen which goes back to around 1820, when the owner at that time had the Four Dogs erected. Documents, not in our possession, but referred to in the manuscript, had evidently been found, containing rumours of a treasure going back to the time of the infamous Judge Jeffreys. The matter was never really treated seriously, since it was not ratified by any other extant manuscripts or historical material.

You may wonder why I did not tell you what I am about to disclose, in the first message I sent.

1) This is the information which our 'friend' in the black overcoat lacks. He knows the other manuscript, but this is the missing 'link' as to the exact whereabouts of the treasure – if there is such a treasure! I could not risk letting him get his hands on it.

2) The information itself is evidently in code and it would be difficult to put it in any other way – as you will see.

All this sounds so complicated but I have tried my best to inform you. As for myself, I am somewhat concerned as to what the Thin Man may do next. This is why I have prepared these two separate messages. I have the unpleasant feeling that he will be calling soon and it will not be to have a friendly discussion as scholars of history!

Here is the missing piece in this complicated jigsaw puzzle! Make of it what you will!

To those who lived within the hall
The key was hidden in the wall.
If you can count to sixty three
A sign within its heart you'll see!

They all looked at one another with puzzled expressions. 'Make of it what you will', he had said. What could they make of it? Once again James broke the silence.

"Surely, we are only going to stand a chance of understanding this when we are in the right place. In other words when presumably we have dug down to wherever the treasure is supposed to be. There are loads of things we don't know, of course. Granny referred to some 'abominable purpose' *Thin Man* and his lot are involved in. We've no idea what that is, but it must be pretty serious and pretty awful for them to do what they've done to Carol and also to Granny himself."

"What do we do now, though?" said Mary. "Do we go to the Four Dogs, perhaps at the weekend and start searching and digging, or do we try to find Granny?"

"It's Saturday tomorrow", said James. "Why don't we ring our parents and check if it's ok for us to stay here at Mary's and then tonight we'll discuss it and decide what to do?"

"Of course, you must stay here, Carol", said Mary, "You'll be safe with us. There's no way that they'll know you're here."

"There's no way I could go home", said Carol, "Thank you so much; I can't tell you how grateful I am."

In no time Mary had rustled up an appetising meal of bacon, egg, mushrooms and baked beans. This was followed by some of her mum's Apple crumble from the fridge, served with lashings of custard. They felt better with a meal inside them and settled down with a cup of coffee to discuss what they should do next.

Thin Man, meanwhile, had a visitor. They too were discussing what to do next. Progress down in the secret cellar was slow. The boys were digging but coming up with nothing. Threats and promises were equally useless. If only they knew that last piece of information. Where was the treasure located? It could be anywhere – it was like looking for a needle in a haystack. Granny was not talking – he would have to be persuaded.

Later that night - the night of the full moon, a lone figure was standing on the flat stone in the centre of the circle of stones in the park. The stones, despite their appearance, as most, if not all people knew, were not of ancient origin. They had been placed there in 1977 to commemorate the visit, for the first time, of the National Eisteddfod of Wales in the town. The Eisteddfod – a Welsh tradition of competition in poetry and music – had links to the ancient Druids, but bore no resemblance to the largely fictitious Druids of Roman times with their supposed human sacrifice and barbaric cruelty.

Sadly, this mysterious person saw the stones as an opportunity to perpetuate some of the worst atrocities attributed, some feel wrongly, to the Druids. In the centre of the circle, on the flat stone, where the Arch-Druid traditionally stood, was this grim, hooded, white-robed figure, with arms upraised toward the moon, in an attitude of worship. Standing sentry-like around the circle of stones were the white-faced *men in black;* their white faces luminescent and ghost-like in the darkness. They were making a low, eerie chanting sound that filled the air with menace.

It was said by G K Chesterton that when men stop believing in God, they don't believe in *nothing* – they believe in *anything.* This strange figure standing in the moonlight somehow believed that he could gain power from the moon and the use of mysterious drugs to bring the world back to the true religion. But strangely – as has always been the case – when the supposed power of such false religion failed, vast wealth, gained by whatever means and the use of force and cruelty would inevitably be used.

Such images may seem rather amusing and even childlike, yet men, sometimes very intelligent men, have ventured down these dark corridors of mystic cruelty and violence to secure their selfish ends. This was the 'abominable purpose' to which Granny had referred – though he was only guessing at what it was. Somewhere in the dim and distant past there was a link, a frightful link, to the man in the centre of the stone circle and the dark unthinkable horrors of the past. His aim, in his madness, was to make them all too terribly present. And the time was approaching fast.

Meanwhile at Mary's house, four Christian young people knelt in prayer. Naïve, pointless, foolish and surely futile, many would have said. But the poet has well said:

More things are wrought by prayer
than this world dreams of!

And they were about to demonstrate the truth of that saying.

CHAPTER 6

THE SHADOW

After the ghostly ritual had ended and the strange participants were making their way into the darkness, one of them paused to remove his macabre outer garment. He smiled grimly to himself, stuffed the garments into a bag and made his way through the trees. *The hour was clearly drawing near and soon it would be time to act.*

As he climbed into the waiting car, the light from the street lamp shone on his face. He was a tall man with a large straggly beard, known to some as Duke! He was *not* involved in plotting a major robbery and he was now no longer in police custody! The police had clearly been deceived. He was no bit-player in some local bank robbery. He must have escaped somehow. One thing was certain; the secret gathering at the stone circle was no fancy dress party. The aims were those of an astute and twisted criminal mind, deeply imbedded in some kind of bizarre covenant with dark forces bent on deception and the destruction of truth and goodness.

Other figures, stealing silently away, were talking breathlessly among themselves as they stopped to reflect on the mystic, magical moment of hypnotic horror and fascination. The unveiling had occurred. They had been present, standing in that circle of stones. They had drunk of the potion, from the sacred cup of enlightenment. Their eyes, staring out from their sockets, bore that glazed look of fascination and fear. *They had seen The Shadow! He had stood before them with arms upraised speaking the words of mystic meaning. They were now the initiated! The Shadow had appeared among them and now victory would be theirs. They had heard of him. His name had been whispered among them, but now they had seen him. Yes, his face had been hidden beneath the white hood of his priestly robe – no one had ever seen his face. But it was The Shadow – there could be no mistake! This was the night of the Shadow!*

Carl Jung once spoke of the *shadow* within each one of us – the potential for evil dwelling in the deep shadows of our minds and hearts. Bondy and his friends had realised that standing in the light and facing the truth is where we meet forgiveness, love and God Himself.

The *Shadow* had not met with God, he had met with Satan, after delving into dark things from the past, occult mysteries that some still pursue in their blindness. The shadow within him had taken over and he was all shadow, but evidently covered over with a veneer of respectability. For, as has been said, 'even the devil transforms himself into an angel of light'. He was convinced that his ancestry went back to the infamous and cruel *Hanging Judge,* who had once lived in the hall. The treasure was loosely supposed to belong to the Judge's family and therefore in his twisted logic it was rightfully his. Judge Jeffreys had meted out 'justice' against rebels who would not conform and it was his mission to bring justice to all who did not follow his twisted way of thinking. Through his evil hypnotic powers he believed he could change them to his way, but if not they would be forced to serve him, or else be destroyed.

There was in his evil philosophy a mixing together of supposed, ancient Druid beliefs, an evil and twisted adaptation of the worship of the Hindu goddess of destruction Kali and a helping of sun and moon worship. Such unbelievable sentiments, far fetched as they may appear, take on a solemn reality when we study those things in our historical past that describe what men have done to achieve their own selfish and evil ambitions. Sadly they are still with us today!

Granny was feeling drowsy. Somehow, he could not remember how, something had been given to him. Oh yes, they had tied him down and injected him with goodness knows what. He remembered being plied with question after question to make him tell them what he knew. Granny looked the image of innocence and weakness, but appearances often deceive! He was a tough old bird and he had been able to resist their efforts to break his resistance through drugs. He vaguely remembered hearing someone say:

"When he comes round, we'll try something rather more persuasive".

Meanwhile at Mary's house a decision had been made and instead of waiting till the next day – Saturday, they had decided to go that night. They would follow the trail from the Four Dogs and try to solve the mystery of the supposed buried treasure. Though Granny was surely in great danger and almost certainly detained in the large mansion seen by Toby and Carol, the key to it all lay in the treasure. That was what *Thin Man* and his cronies were after. If Bondy & co. could locate it, they would hold the whip hand, Carol stayed in the house where she felt safe and could recover from her recent ordeal. They told her if she felt it necessary, should there appear to be any threat from the enemy, she should phone the police and mention Bondy's name. The doors were all securely locked and being a wealthy business man the property was also fitted out with the latest security devices.

They set off in the dark and headed for the well known local landmark known as the Four Dogs. There was no one about and there was a full moon. They paced out as well as they could the four hundred metres from the entrance where the gates to the driveway had once stood. The spot they reached was surrounded by a small clump of trees. Nearby there were modern apartments, their cosy, homely atmosphere contrasting strongly with the mystery and tension that gripped the minds of the youngsters. There was nothing that suggested the presence nearby of some magical entrance to a dark, hidden recess containing an ancient treasure.

Switching on their torches they began to search for something, anything that might betray a way down. Since Granny had mentioned 'digging', they had brought with them a couple of spades. The area where they were standing inside the clump of trees was, as might be expected, covered with grass. They decided to test the ground to see whether it would yield any suggestion of something unusual below the surface. Suddenly, as they were about to wonder whether they were on another wild goose chase, Toby's spade hit something solid. They crowded round, shining their torches on the spot where he was scraping away the surface grass and accumulated dirt.

Slowly, but surely, a solid stone slab appeared, measuring about three feet square. Toby tested it with his foot – it seemed very solid, never moving at all. What was it? Could this be the spot, they wondered? The question was, would it move or lift? It would have to, if beneath it was some sort of entrance down below ground. James knelt down and began to rub with his hand the surface of the stone slab. They heard his sharp intake of breath!

"Look", he said. "Look at this!"

They all knelt down to examine the spot towards which his finger was pointing. There was a clear imprint in the stone and Toby was the first to come up with an explanation.

"It's like part of a dog or cat's paw", he said. "When this was concreted a dog or a cat must have walked on it while it was still wet and left part of its paw mark."

"No, it's not that", said Mary. "I don't know what it is but it's not that. And anyway, remember this is a stone slab, not a piece of concrete. Look, it's solid stone."

"You're right", said James. "It is solid stone and pretty old at that, I would say. It's not an animal's paw either, but I think I know what it is. Remember I've been studying the Druids for my course work and I think this is an ancient symbol of the Druids, a sort of mystic sign. And if I'm right then I think we're onto something!"

CHAPTER 7

PERIL UNDERGROUND

The three of them were staring at the strange symbol in the stone. It looked a bit like the three middle fingers on a human hand, spread wide apart and pointing downwards. Their thoughts soon went back to the stone itself. Their hearts pounded with anticipation and also fear.

"The question is; can we lift it?" said Mary, frowning as she guessed at the weight of it.

Toby placed his spade at the edge of the slab and began to work it underneath, to see if he could prise it up. It didn't seem to be moving, so James joined him with his spade, while Mary looked on encouragingly. They pushed down, leaning on the spades and straining every muscle in their efforts. Then they heard a slight groaning, scraping sound and saw just the slightest movement. Toby, used to training with heavy weights for his boxing, heaved with all his might, leaning on the spade and pushing downwards.

"It's moving", said Mary excitedly. "Keep going, keep going!"

They kept going, the beads of sweat dripping down their faces and glistening in the light of the torch, held by Mary.

At last a gap appeared beneath the solid slab of stone which must have been about six inches thick. Mary quickly picked up a thick branch of a tree lying nearby on the ground. Swiftly she wedged it underneath the gap, pushing it right across the length of the slab. They stopped for a breather.

"Phew, that took some shifting", said Toby. "At least that proves nobody else has been down here recently – assuming there is a 'down here'".

He shone his torch into the hole and then whispered excitedly:

"It definitely goes further down!"

"Let's see if we can move this thing across and make the entrance clear", said James, reaching down and taking hold of the slab.

All three leaned their weight against the slab and slowly manoeuvred it to one side. They shone their torches down into the darkness. All three gasped in unison.

The light from the torches revealed a flight of stone steps winding downward in a spiral. They looked at each other in astonishment and also fear. *What lay beneath? Where would the spiral stairs lead?* There was only one way to find out. James led the way, with Mary in the middle and Toby bringing up the rear. The stairway descended steeply and they had to proceed with great caution not only because of the steepness, but also because the steps were wet and extremely slippery. Each step was a step into the unknown and into thick darkness. Then to James's astonishment he came to what had to be a dead end. Suddenly he was face to face with a brick wall. There was no way forward and no turning to right or left. Whatever purpose this strange stairway had served, the way through had evidently at some time been bricked in.

"It's a dead end", whispered James as the other two stood there, waiting to move forward.

He shone his torch all around the wall facing him in the hope of finding some clue; anything to explain why they should have come to this abrupt end. They heard him gasp and whisper hoarsely:

"I've found something – another of those Druid signs. Perhaps it means something. He shone his torch onto the brick containing an identical sign to the one they had seen on the stone slab. He reached up and touched the brick – hoping it would trigger something off. He pushed again – harder this time. It moved! But it wasn't only the brick that moved! A section of the wall moved – about three feet square of it - and before them stood an opening wide enough for them to crawl through. They hesitated, James holding them back with an urgently outstretched arm. They could see why, for ahead of them was a tiny balcony and beyond that down below at a deeper level was a room. The room was lit with candles and they could hear the sound of activity and muffled voices.

Switching off their torches at a signal from James, they followed as he clambered carefully onto the small balcony from which descended another, much smaller stairway to the floor below. From there an archway would afford them entry into the candle-lit room. Hardly daring to breathe James led the way down the stairway to the floor and they tip-toed across the floor to the archway. Peering round the corner they found themselves looking into a fairly large area, like a sort of underground cellar. It was lit by seven large candles, placed in specially prepared alcoves. There was clearly no electricity in there and, thought James, smiling to himself – no en suite facilities! The smile faded however as he took in the activity of the room and the occupants. There were four young boys around fifteen years of age stripped to the waist and digging into the dirt floor of the room.

The room was obviously ancient and the dank smell was relieved only by the smell of the burning candles. Two men stood sentry-like on either side of the room. They were huge brutes – like the one Toby had described who had guarded Carol. They carried long, thick poles and from time to time smacked the poles threateningly into the palms of their massive hands.

"It looks like some sort of slave labour", whispered Mary.

"And I bet they're digging for treasure", whispered Toby from behind.

"What are we going to do? That's what I want to know", said James.

"Perhaps we should watch and wait – and maybe pray", replied Mary.

"We could certainly do with some help – divine or otherwise", said James grimly as he looked at the two men. Then Toby let out a hoarse cry as he stared more closely at the young boys:

"James", he said. "Those boys, I recognise them. They are the missing boys from the estate. The other missing ones were found and the reason for their absence was discovered to be fairly innocent. These four were the only ones unaccounted for and the police thought they would just turn up like the rest. I can't believe it!"

"Maybe a few things are fitting into place", replied James grimly, "and I'm not sure I like the way they fit".

Just then Toby gripped James by the arm:

"Somebody's coming, I'm sure of it."

James and Mary peered back into the candle-lit room.

"No", said Toby. "Behind us - I'm sure I heard a footstep on the stair, someone's coming up behind us.

They froze on the spot, turning their heads anxiously. Who could it be and why or how could they be coming down the stairway? They began to feel a sickly panic rising inside their stomachs.

A figure emerged, peering through the gap in the opened wall. It was a man they recognised and whom they had once thought of as a friend. Now they knew he was part of the sinister gang with the black suits and the ghostly face-masks. It was the man they knew as Duke, not wearing his sinister gear but acting the part of the friendly vagrant. They were trapped!

CHAPTER 8

LIGHTS OUT!

"We're sunk", said Mary in a hoarse whisper.

James was fingering his catapult, fastened to the belt around his waist and brought along as usual in case of emergencies, along with the leather pouch containing carefully selected stones.

Meanwhile Duke, if that was his real name, was stealthily making his way down the steps. As he reached the bottom and his eyes adjusted to the darkness, he spotted the trio ahead of him, even though they pressed themselves against the dark wall. He was walking steadily towards them in a determined fashion, a smile of seeming triumph on his face. He had found them!

With a sigh, Bondy reached for his catapult and began fitting a stone from his pouch. He turned with feet apart to face the oncoming traitor, raising his catapult to take aim.

"Oh no", cried Mary, "he's got a gun in his hand?"

Duke was now striding towards them his right arm outstretched, pointing in their direction!

"Is it a gun? It could be a gun", whispered Mary again.

As he drew ever nearer they could see that for some reason he had his finger pressed firmly over his lips as if to silence them. *Who was he kidding? Did he think they were going to fall for the friendly neighbourhood tramp ploy? Not this time.*

Quickly, James shone his torch directly into the face of the advancing Duke. Toby braced himself and stood with fists clenched and feet apart, ready for action.

He was now just a few yards from them, the beam from the torch lighting up his face and also the card held firmly in his right hand.

"It's ok kids", he whispered, smiling widely and raising his hands high in the air as if they were pointing a gun at him. "Here, James", he said, handing him the card and then to emphasise that he was no threat to them, returning both his hands to their raised position above his head. "Don't shoot, I'm innocent, honest!" His eyes were fixed on the slightly raised catapult in James's hand.

James looked at the card and read out slowly and deliberately two words on it: *Detective Sergeant.* They all looked at each other, lost for words.

He was not lost for words and still smiling broadly but keeping his voice low he responded to their puzzled, questioning looks:

"I've been following you lot for days! You do get about don't you? But am I glad I've finally caught up with you!"

They were still looking dumbfounded and kept glancing at one another for some sort of assurance that they were hearing things correctly.

"So who are you?" asked Mary in a hoarse whisper, frowning and spreading her hands wide for emphasis.

He told them that his real name was Clutton – Michael Clutton – in fact Detective Sergeant

Michael Clutton. He apologised for the deception and the phoney arrest.

"The inspector regretted having to deceive you, but it had to be, under the circumstances." Then he stopped abruptly. "Look, this is no time for lengthy explanations; we've got urgent business to see to. I went undercover and infiltrated the 'ghost squad' in the weird get-up, so I know what's going on over there." He pointed to the candle-lit cellar with the diggers. "But I didn't know about the secret passage. I just followed you. Inspector Roberts said 'Follow Bondy' – so I did and here I am."

"They've got Granny, my old history teacher", said Bondy.

"And we're pretty sure they've got him in that grand looking mansion not far from the old Jeffreys road", said Toby.

"Well if my guess is correct, from what I've been able to glean while under cover with the ghost squad, there should be a passageway from that house to this ancient cellar. It would be an ideal way for us to get in, but first we've got to get past those two ugly looking brutes. And no, in case you're asking I don't have a gun and they look a pretty tough pair of twins."

"What if we could put the lights out? Maybe we could tackle them in the dark and with the element of surprise." James was fingering his catapult again.

The detective peered round the corner of the archway and frowned darkly. "I've just counted seven candles round the room and each one of them high up in an alcove. There's no way we can get to all seven of them without being seen, so we can forget that one!"

"We could get to them with this", said James, grinning broadly and holding up his catapult.

"You can't be serious", said the detective, looking at James as though he had taken leave of his senses.

"Oh yes he is!" replied Toby gleefully. "Just wait till you see him in action."

"It's true", said Mary, giving James a big hug. "He's a genius with that catapult."

The detective looked on in amazement: "You don't say? You really mean it? Inspector Roberts never told me you possessed a "Lethal Weapon". He grinned once more as he spoke.

"My aim would be to extinguish all the candles in quick succession so that the room would be plunged into darkness before they could react. The element of surprise should do it." James looked the detective in the eyes as he spoke.

Toby could not resist; "They'll think there's been a power cut!" he whispered, holding his hand over his mouth to stifle the giggle, while the detective held up his hands in admiration.

"You amaze me, you three. I didn't really believe what the inspector said about you. But now I'm a believer, I guess. So, go on show me!"

After a brief discussion on their plan of action after 'lights out', Bondy fitted the first stone to his catapult and then placed the remaining six stones on the flat top of the wall. Fortunately the cellar in which the treasure hunting was taking place was slightly below them. He was looking down from a strategic place for accurate shooting. What took place next left the detective open-mouthed.

Like some sort of well-oiled machine, after that first stone had whizzed through the dark cellar and extinguished the first candle, Bondy had swept up the remaining stones and fitted and fired them with blinding speed, one after the other. 'Plop, plop, plop'..., seven times. Seven candles, seven shots and the cellar plunged into thickest darkness. *Everywhere went silent. The digging stopped. The two thugs ceased their arrogant, boasting chatter in mid-sentence. The only sound was the steady drip, drip, of the water running down the walls of the damp, smelly cellar. Toby was right – it was as if there had been a power cut!*

In the darkness, four silent, ghostly figures crept, all unseen, behind the unsuspecting guards. The detective stole up behind the first one, snatched the club from his hand and with one swift blow brought the club down upon his unguarded head. He slumped to the ground unconscious. The other thug turned and was about to move to the attack when he was met by a thunderbolt as Toby head-butted him in the stomach and knocked him flying over the crouching form of Bondy, kneeling just behind him. His head hit the cellar wall and he too slumped to the floor – out for the count. Meanwhile Mary had climbed up to the nearest candle and brought it down to the detective who struck a match and lit it. Toby quickly turned to the astonished boys, cowering in fear in the darkness. "Hey you guys, it's me, Toby from the estate. We're the advance rescue party. You're free!"

CHAPTER 9

THE SECRET TUNNEL

They found some rope lying in a corner and Michael tied up the two guards and gagged them with some old rags conveniently discovered on the cellar floor.

"We're short of nothing we've got", was Toby's amusing comment as the boys from the estate gathered round him. To them he was already something of a local hero on account of his boxing achievements. He was one of them – a local kid from the estate, who had overcome problems with drugs and drink and made good. Now his 'street cred.' in their sight had shot up a hundred times. They all embraced each other, joyfully, slapping one another on the back and laughing in relief.

"How did the lights go out?"- asked one of them, looking totally mystified by the whole incident.

Toby simply pointed to Bondy, who held up his catapult with a slightly embarrassed smile on his face. All four former captives whistled loudly in amazement.

"It's true", said the detective. "I can vouch for it, though I don't think I would have believed it if I hadn't seen it with my own eyes."

He introduced himself and there were introductions all round, after which the boys briefly told the story of their enticement into the spider's web of the *Thin Man.*

"I think we've learned a lesson", said one of them. "We realise now we were fools to listen to all that talk of easy money and fun and fantasy. It seemed great at first but then came the sting."

Another one nodded grimly: "Yeah, it did seem great at first – you know, like, all that booze and money to spend and all that sort of stuff. But it got scary later and we realised we were trapped. I think they were going to get rid of us if they had to. We were idiots and I guess I'm not as hard as I thought I was."

"They're desperate for that treasure", said a third. "They'll stop at nothing, I bet."

"An' I tell you what too; they're dead scared of that man in the black coat, an' they're all even more scared of the other guy. He came once, looking like somebody from the Klu Klux Klan or whatever they call it. He was weird, real weird," the fourth youngster burst in with his eyes flashing.

"I've seen him recently in his sort of priestly get-up", said Michael. "But we don't know who he is. They call him *The Shadow.*"

He went on to tell them of his strange and disturbing experience on the night when they gathered around the Druid stones in the park. He told them how he had infiltrated the sect and had stood there under the full moon, horrified by the hypnotic terror of the atmosphere.

"Yeah, they called him *The Shadow* and they practically worshipped him. He had some sort of power over them. I've seen some bad things in my time, but I was scared, I can tell you."

Apparently the detective had been pursuing this *Shadow* across the continent in conjunction with Interpol. There were links with strange sects in other countries. They knew he was in this country without getting any clear sight of him. He had links with USA and also India. There were suspicions that he was heading up some sort of international or even global occult movement aiming at world dominance. The trouble was they could never pin the movement down to anything illegal. There was always this outward veneer of respectability around the gatherings of the cult.

"My guess is he's actually a foreigner from India or somewhere like that." The audience listened fascinated and also disturbed.

Meanwhile James was hearing echoes of his *War of the Worlds* track: *'The chances of anything coming from Mars are a million to one he said, but still they come........who would have believed.....who could have dreamed..........as they drew their plans against us.'* No, he thought, not from Mars, but truly evil.

Then he shook himself out of his nightmarish dream and spoke urgently to the detective. "Michael, excuse me interrupting, but there's something we must do which must now not be delayed. I mentioned before that our old history teacher is being held in the house at the end of this tunnel. I dread to think what'll happen to him if he doesn't reveal to them the information they're so desperate to obtain."

The detective nodded and they began instantly to move forward, guided by the four youngsters. The secret passageway had become so tragically familiar to them. As they made their way by torchlight James filled in the details about Granny and the code.

"So you actually have the secret code relating to the treasure?" the detective asked.

"Trouble is", replied James, "it's in this funny rhyme and we don't know what it's on about."

"But at least you've got it and that could be a good bargaining tool if it comes down to that." The detective scratched his nose thoughtfully as they continued along the dark passageway. "I think, James, there are a few more twists and turns before we're through with this and the danger isn't over yet by a long way."

The tunnel seemed endless, but eventually one of the boys indicated that they were drawing near to the point where the tunnel entered the house. Some steps appeared ahead of them and as they drew closer they saw a trap door at the top of the steps.

"It opens into the wine cellar", explained the previous spokesman, pointing up to the trap door. "Then there's a door at the other end of the cellar which takes you into the kitchen – up some more steps. That's where the domestic staff will be."

The detective led the way as they ascended the steps. Then one by one, they each entered the wine cellar, keeping as quiet as possible. The trap door was carefully shut and moving with extreme caution they proceeded past row after row of vast quantities of wine, till they reached the kitchen door.

They could hear the sound of muffled voices from inside – the occupants were obviously having a cup of tea and just relaxing after eating a meal. Occasionally they heard the sound of loud laughter, the clinking of cups and the scraping of chairs on the stone floor. The detective crept up the stairs, motioning the others to wait in silence at the bottom while he checked out the situation.

Holding his breath, he turned the handle of the door. The group down below him instinctively screwed up their faces awaiting a possible creaking sound as the door swung slowly on its hinges. There was to their horror a slight creak – but just at that moment another loud outburst of laughter drowned the sound to the ears of those in the kitchen. *Phew!*

Through the crack created in the doorway he was able to take in the main details and layout of the room. It was a large kitchen, rather old in its design, as you might expect. There were long wooden tables on either side of the room, where various kinds of preparations would have taken place. Down the middle of the room was another long table around which four members of the domestic staff were sitting. At one end of the room there was a grand looking, large oven, set in the wall, big enough it seemed to cook the 'fatted calf' that welcomed home the prodigal son in the bible story. No cooking was going on however. There were two men and two women chatting happily and drinking cups of either tea or coffee. *How to get past them without raising the alarm? That was the question.*

Michael crept back down the stairs, leaving the door just slightly ajar. In a hoarse whisper he briefly outlined the situation to the group waiting anxiously below and the problem it posed. After some silent thought, it was, perhaps unsurprisingly, Toby who had the bright idea.

"Why don't we send the boys here, into the kitchen, bursting in all excited and telling them to come quickly because the treasure has been found. They'll know the boys and associate them with digging for the treasure. We'll be waiting at the bottom of the steps, hiding round the side. When they've gone down the stairs and are making for the trap door, the boys will turn round and run back to join us. Then we're in!"

Michael grinned and added excitedly. "There's a key in the door, I noticed, so we can lock them in the wine cellar. They'll come to no real harm, I'm sure and there's plenty of wine down there if they get thirsty!"

Everybody nodded their agreement and slapped Toby on the back in appreciation of his smart thinking.

At a sign from the detective the four boys ran up the steps and burst into the kitchen shouting and yelling excitedly. They stopped, gasping for breath as if they had just come running up the length of the passageway. The occupants of the room jumped up from their seats in alarm, turning to stare at the intruders.

"Quick", cried the boy in the front, "it's the treasure. We've found it. You'll never believe it, come and see!"

They did believe it and dashing from the table, they made for the door, led by the four boys, who were by now really acting out the part and rather enjoying themselves. This was one way of getting some sort of revenge against their captors. Scrambling down the steps in pursuit of the boys, once down the steps they raced ahead of them in their eagerness. They were soon lifting the trap door and clambering down more steps, oblivious to the fact that the four boys had not followed them.

The boys arrived back at the kitchen door to find the others waiting for them. Everybody was grinning. It had worked perfectly. They quickly entered the kitchen, locked the cellar door behind them and made for the other door at the far end of the room. The detective opened it cautiously, stepping into a long dark corridor which clearly led away from the servants' quarters to the main and much grander section of the house. The vast corridor was adorned with expensive looking old paintings. They were hanging on ornately wood-panelled walls which shone brightly from a recent polishing. They could smell the polish!

"Whoever owns this place must be worth a bit." Toby whispered hoarsely.

After some time they were approaching a large beautifully crafted oak doorway, matching exactly the impressive wall panelling. Their feet were making scarcely any sound at all on the thickly carpeted floor, but the detective held up his hand and pressed it to his lips signalling total silence as they neared the door. Despite the thickness of the oak door they could just about hear the sound of voices from within the room. This time however the voices were much clearer. It was obvious that the occupants, unlike the domestic staff, were not engaged in idle chit-chat over a cup of tea. There was an ominous solemnity about the tone of the voices that filtered through the doorway. They were being raised at times to a high fever pitch, indicating anger, frustration and threat.

CHAPTER 10

RESCUE

Bondy was convinced he could recognise at least two of the voices. One of them containing a threatening tone was unmistakably *Thin Man!* The other voice he could not be absolutely sure of, because it was at times barely audible, as if the speaker was under some sort of terrible stress, or even in pain. And yet by a kind of frightful and inevitable logic, he somehow knew that the voice belonged to his beloved history teacher – Granny.

With a sign to the detective James indicated his desire to come to the front. He moved forward as the detective nodded his approval, crouching down in front of the door and taking hold carefully of the large round door handle. Once again all faces were screwed up in tense anticipation of a dreaded squeak or creak. The consequences this time would prove far graver than on the previous occasion.

Slowly, with his bottom lip between his teeth – which always, for some reason, seemed to help in this kind of situation – James turned the cumbersome handle to the right. When he was sure that the latch had cleared the hole of the door jamb, he began ever so gently to push the door very, very slightly ajar. It was open just enough for him to see into the room. *No creaks, thank God!*

The room, into which he was now peering through the crack in the doorway, was once again of similar decor to that observed along the corridor. Beautifully carpeted; with oak-panelled walls, finely carved furniture, a massively long solid oak table in the middle of the room; eight matching chairs placed strategically around it and plush, luxurious easy chairs at the far end of the room near some bookcases. *That's where the guests retire to for coffee and liqueurs thought James.*

Suddenly, his eyes lit upon the occupants of the room. There were three men, standing several metres from the door through which he was peering. They had their backs to him leaving the one, remaining, lone figure; he was facing the door and sitting on a hard chair, not designed for comfort. *It was Granny!* And he was not drinking coffee or liqueurs. In fact he looked as though he had not had anything substantial to eat or drink for some considerable time. He looked pale and haggard, his normally cheerful countenance now clouded and his eyes downcast. At a sign from one of the men another from the group stepped over to the prisoner – for that was what he clearly was. Although he did not appear to be bound in any way, it was as if his spirit had been broken and all strength had left his body.

The rest of the onlookers had now crowded round the door and as best they could were looking in upon the disturbing scene. The stranger who was standing behind Granny appeared to be of Indian origin, with dark swarthy features. He wore a turban and beneath it was a sharply pointed nose and piercing, cruel eyes that seemed to flash and glint like some kind of warning light in a danger area.

Below his thin insensitive lips he wore a black, pointed beard. Standing now behind Granny's chair he was also facing the door through which he was being observed. He was looking straight ahead of him, staring hypnotically across the room. So strong and compelling was his gaze that the hidden intruders ducked instinctively behind the door. It was as if he could see them and knew of their presence.

Swiftly, they gathered themselves and turned their gaze back upon the desperate scene, daring to look again. They saw him take from somewhere inside the folds of his long garment, a silk scarf. He held it almost lovingly in his hands, running his fingers through the silken smoothness. Then quickly he stretched it to its full length and in an instant, quick as a flash, transferred it over Granny's head and round his neck. He began moving it back and forth along Granny's throat, his face a picture of sinister pleasure and enjoyment. A voice spoke from the midst of the watching tormentors. Whoever it was he appeared to be in charge.

"Mr Davies, please be reasonable, we do not wish to hurt you further, but we must have the information about the treasure."

He then addressed the Indian in Hindi – the language of northern India. He responded instantly. With two swift movements obviously the result of regular practice, he wound the scarf round both hands, thus shortening it and then began to tighten it around Granny's throat, jerking his head back with considerable force.

James could not restrain the stark horror and disgust that shot through his body like an electric shock, nor the word he blurted out in a hoarse whisper:

Thuggee! Thuggee! It sounded so loud to him that he thought Granny's tormentors must have heard it. Evidently they had not. His mind was working overtime as he remembered Granny's history lessons about the campaign of the British Government in India against the cult of *Thuggee,* in the mid 1800s, when it was finally put down. These sinister professional assassins were worshippers of the Hindu goddess Kali who was associated with death and destruction. They ritually murdered travellers as offerings to the goddess, by means of strangulation with a silk scarf. Bondy's mind was in a whirl: *Someone's twisted and perverted mind was reviving the cult in some way – and here in this country!*

He forced himself to look again into the room, fearful that the sight that would meet his eyes would be utterly unbearable. To his relief the scarf had been removed once more from Granny's neck. His head was slumped forward again, but a slight movement indicated that he was still alive. They were playing with him – the monsters! The horrified spectators looked at one another, desperation written on every face. *What could they do?*

The thug – for that is where we get the name from – was placing the scarf around Granny's neck again, when detective Michael turned to Bondy, gripping his arm so fiercely that it hurt:

"We're going to stop that.............!" (He used a familiar term of abuse which indicated his suspicions regarding the legitimacy of the Indian's parentage!) and then: "Let's go Bondy!"

As one man, acting in total unison, without any planned instructions, they charged into the room. The horror of what they were witnessing united them and moulded them into a troop of commandos bent on justice for the oppressed victim. Bondy's catapult was already fitted with a stone.

"Police, police!" cried Michael as he led the charge, followed by Bondy, Mary, Toby and the rest.

The thug was just about to tighten the scarf when a stone from Bondy's catapult smashed into his wrist and with a scream of pain he dropped the vile instrument of death, looking up with fury and hatred in his eyes. But at the same moment he was struck on the point of the jaw by a fierce blow from the detective's fist. He fell to the floor dazed and struggling for consciousness.

Meanwhile Toby had grabbed *Thin Man* who was about to escape through the door at the far end of the room. He fought furiously but was no match for Toby, whose mind was filled with the thoughts of the cruelty meted out to his precious Carol. It ended up with Toby sitting on him as he lay face down on the ground, both arms twisted up behind his back.

The third occupant had evaded the four youngsters, and Mary was unable to prevent him escaping through the door. He was dressed in some sort of priestly garment and wore a mask and a hood which obscured his face completely. He had to be *The Shadow.*

"He's the one", shouted Michael. "We *must* get him; we *must* get him this time!" He was just finishing handcuffing the other two, but Bondy was after him, surging forward as he did in his sprint races. He shot through the door, just in time to see the mysterious figure rounding the corner of the long corridor.

He heard the door slam as he sped after him, skidding at the corner and bursting through the door in hot pursuit. He could see him scampering down the steps at the front of the house where a car stood waiting, his long priestly robe flowing out behind him. Bondy went into overdrive, straining every muscle, his face flushed with anger as well as effort and the thought of what might have happened if they had been too late.

He must catch him; he just had to. If not, he could be gone for good. He was gaining on him as his quarry drew near to the car. The car door opened and the man leapt in, the engine roaring to life instantly, just as Bondy was reaching out desperately to grab something, anything. But he was too late. He skidded to a halt as the car disappeared down the drive. He bent double, gasping for breath, his chest heaving as he stared in disbelief. He had been so close!

When he had recovered his breath, he turned slowly and made his way back up the steps, dragging his feet, partly from disappointment and partly from sheer weariness after his desperate effort. Then remembering Granny and his awful ordeal, he began to quicken his steps to join the others in the mansion that looked so grand, but hid such horrors.

CHAPTER 11

CATCHING A SHADOW?

Higgins was puzzled and afraid. He had not expected to see *The Shadow* coming tearing down the steps and demanding to be driven in his car. That was not normally his job. He'd never done this before! He didn't like it. It was bad enough driving the other one around – the one with the sharp pointed walking stick. He grimaced and felt his neck where that very same walking stick had pressed forcefully against his skin. He'd heard about the so called *Shadow*, seen glimpses of him from a distance – now he was in his car. Good grief! What next? Usually he just came and went – well, like a shadow. No one knew where he lived or how he came and went. He rarely spoke and when he did it was sometimes in a foreign language. And he never usually spoke to Higgins. He'd spoken to him just before – and it wasn't in a foreign language either. He'd screamed at him to open the door and put his foot down fast. Higgins had never seen him in such a hurry; always seemed in such control of everything. Funny that! Who was that chasing him? - Strange.

He looked in the mirror as he approached the end of the long winding drive and saw a masked face gazing at him. He shuddered and then wondered whether he should smile and ask how his passenger was or make some comment about the weather. He decided against it. Then he heard just one word of command as he reached the end of the drive: "Left."

He quickly turned left, almost forgetting to check whether any traffic was coming, in his haste to do the bidding of the masked man. He noticed that his passenger kept turning and looking through the rear window for signs of pursuit and occasionally, through the side windows as if to get his bearings. Higgins turned his attention back onto the road and concentrated on his driving.

"Stop here."

The sudden imperious command made Higgins jump in alarm, so much so, that he stamped rather heavily on his brakes causing the car to lurch and jerk to a stop in a lay-by. He watched nervously as his menacing passenger climbed out and headed for the woods at the side of the road. He found himself staring at the silently retreating figure as he began to enter the woods. Then he nearly jumped out of his skin when the man suddenly turned round and spotting the driver's keen interest in his activities, waved his arms angrily indicating in no uncertain manner that he should leave *instantly.*

Higgins quickly put the car into first gear and with a roar and a screech of tyres, shot off like a rocket, only just avoiding the car behind him. It was just overtaking him, horn blaring loudly. The masked figure never took his eyes off the disappearing car until it had gone completely out of sight round the next bend.

Deep inside the woods, the outer, priestly garments and the mask were removed and placed in a bag taken from some bushes. Then carrying the bag he walked further into the wood until he finally disappeared into its dark depths.

James arrived back at the house to find a scene of relative calm. He heard the sound of an ambulance alarm in the distance. He crouched down anxiously beside the frail form of his old history teacher. He was comforted by the thought of its imminent arrival. Granny was barely conscious, but Michael assured Bondy that in his opinion, though he was clearly in need of medical attention, he should be okay.

He had already contacted the back-up team on his phone and they were on their way to the other entrance by which Bondy & co had entered earlier. He was reckoning that by now the domestic staff would have freed the two guards. They would have guessed that there had to be some other way in and would be trying to make their escape. Later he was relieved to discover that the back-up had arrived just in time to catch the two guards and the other staff as they emerged from its depths. They were met by a sizeable armed police squad who had not had too much difficulty in arresting them and holding them for further questioning.

So far so good but there were still two outstanding problems. The main one was, of course, the identity and capture of the key figure in the whole horrific mystery. The mysterious *Shadow* was still at large.

"We must nip this thing in the bud before it grows here and develops into something beyond control. While he is at large we cannot rest." Michael was looking with deadly serious intent into the eyes of the group of rescuers following the arrival of the back-up team. They had now taken the handcuffed and crestfallen prisoners, loaded them into the waiting police van and sped off down the drive. He continued:

"We have seen tonight the unbelievable potential for evil in these people. They must be stopped and this *Shadow* is the key to it all. He clearly has an insane passion for dominance over people and like others before him he believes his dominance can reach national and even international proportions. It may sound far-fetched and even laughable, but it is far from that. This man is serious and he'll evidently stop at nothing. If we don't get him, he'll be back to his own country in India or somewhere and we may never get another chance like this."

Bondy had got the number plate of the black saloon car, but when he mentioned it, Toby was able to confirm that it was the same one he and Alfie had chased before. It seemed to be more linked to *Thin Man* than the *Shadow*. However, they all agreed that the driver of that car could have important information. They must keep a look out for him and the police would be combing the area for any sightings.

The other thing was the small matter of the supposed hidden treasure – evidently important enough to torture and kill for. Although the treasure was not high on their priority list, the big question was, would the mysterious *Shadow* try again to get it? What manpower did he now have to aid him in such an attempt? He had lost the services of the occupants of the house, but Michael knew that there were others and potentially a considerable number. On that night when the *Shadow* had made his appearance in the park, Michael had been there as part of the crowd. And there had been some crowd! The mansion and the secret entrance would have to be guarded.

There was another serious question to ask in relation to the treasure. Was there still therefore a risk to Bondy & co and Carol, since they now had in their possession the final piece of manuscript which would reveal the whereabouts of the treasure? Of course it was possible that the *Shadow* would now attempt, as quickly and as silently as possible, to escape or lay low for a while. They just didn't know. Who was he anyway? Maybe the Thugee-man would tell the police, under interrogation – that is if he knew. Michael was pretty sure that, like the wielder of the silk scarf, he also was Indian. But the monster had always kept his identity secret and they doubted whether anyone knew who he was or where he came from. The conclusion they came to was that they must try at all costs to find the dreaded *Shadow.* That wasn't going to be easy and it could be very risky. After all the question was: *How do you catch a Shadow? Maybe you end up just, as the saying goes, 'chasing shadows'?*

The next day was Sunday and the first thing on Bondy & co's minds was to go to their special church. This they did and later on, feeling encouraged and inspired, as they made their way to Toby's house, they were discussing the whole thing together. They'd prayed about it earlier and felt sure that a way would be found to track down the missing, elusive, *Shadow.* Harry, of course had missed out on all the excitement, but was really fired up by all they had told him. He suddenly blurted out his feelings on the matter: "I bet I could find him! – You know me, I can find out anything."

They all stopped in their tracks and looked at the earnest expression on Harry's face. James was the first to speak:

"Do you know, I believe you could be right and I'll tell you why, Harry, you too are a shadow, not in the evil sense in which he is, but because you used to live in the shadows. You were a compulsive 'eavesdropper', suddenly appearing outside somebody's window and then melting into the background as if you'd never been there in the first place.

I know we've tried to cure you of the bad aspects of it, but this is just what we need. You missed out on the action before, but now you're going to be right in the middle of it. You've helped us in the past and now you're going to help us again."

Harry's face burst into a huge grin as they all stood looking at him in admiration. He felt good!

"When do I start, boss?" he asked, standing to attention with his arms by his sides.

"Right away", replied Bondy, putting an affectionate arm around his shoulder, "and the sooner the better."

Harry required no instructions apart from the need for him to keep in touch with James on a regular basis. What he did was instinctive – even inspired. His senses were fine-tuned for 'nosing out' suspicious or dangerous activity. He had learned his art in the hard school of life when it had been necessary for him to fend for himself, either to keep away from his violent father or to find solace from the pain of a loveless mother. He knew the area like the back of his hand, having wandered for hours in all sorts of places he would never normally have gone. He knew all the short cuts, all the hiding places and all the best places to find out things nobody was supposed to know. In his own special way, Harry was a genius! So once again, Harry began to wander. *The Shadow now had a shadow!*

CHAPTER 12

ME AND MY SHADOW!

He was troubled; after all things had not exactly gone according to plan. They had been so close, but now things were going to be difficult. Yet there was still a chance. He had escaped and that was the main thing. No one knew who he was, so he could never be traced. The question was, should he leave the country? That could be difficult, simply because of the watching police and security forces. But it was not at all impossible. He was always careful and meticulous in his planning. Perhaps it would after all be better to go and pursue his plans elsewhere. But...there was the treasure. *Ah yes the treasure!*

The treasure was rightfully his. He had traced his ancestry back to the infamous Judge of the 'Bloody Assize'. The mansion also was his with its secret underground passageway leading to the cellar beneath where the Old Hall had once stood. He had no idea who had opened the passageway from the mansion, but he had found it some years ago and it had confirmed his suspicions that the mansion had, as his research indicated, at one time been associated with the Judge.

He was linked to that cruel family and yet, in his mind what the judge had done was not cruel. He had simply meted out justice to foolish and wicked rebels. It was not cruelty but simply justice. People were in rebellion today too and needed either changing or else overthrowing, or even destroying. Strong dynamic leaders were a thing of the past and authority must be restored. The gods of death and destruction still needed appeasing when the world went astray. He was reviving ancient Druid beliefs and a return to the gods of the earth and nature, allied with the great goddess Kali, with whom he had formed an alliance in India. Such power could not be opposed. He would win in the end – it was written in the stars and history bore witness to such power.

If only he had been able to get that information, the treasure would surely now be his. He must try again! He had access to wealth, but with those surely untold riches, his influence would increase and the spread of his occult, mystical power would be almost unstoppable. *These were the thoughts of the Shadow as he pondered the effects of the recent setback.*

His thinking differed very little from that of all tyrants and megalomaniacs down the ages. The lofty thoughts and grandiose schemes of men have always been rather overdone. And man in his pride and arrogance forgets that the simplest thing can overturn the most complex plans. It was said of Alexander the Great that when he had conquered the greater part of the then known world, he wept because there was nothing else to conquer. Unfortunately for him he died quite unexpectedly after a night of feasting and drunken carousing. Further conquests abruptly ended! So what stood in the way of the *Shadow,* this would-be tyrant, supposed distant relative of the 'Hanging Judge of the Bloody Assize', of whom it was said that he was perpetually drunk or in a rage?

His name was Harry, rather a small boy of no great academic achievement, but highly qualified in the tough university of life. Yes, he was street-wise and more aware than most of reality in the raw. He was some opponent, though to look at him, no one would have given him a chance! Harry was to the *Shadow* what David in the bible was to Goliath the giant – and we know how that ended!

Of course, Harry was on the lookout for the black saloon car. Bondy had told him about it and given him the number plate. Harry was going to find it. This he was convinced he could do.

Higgins meanwhile had gone back later that fateful night to spy out the situation at the mansion. He had no idea of what had really happened. He parked the car somewhere out of sight and crept through the trees to a point where he had a good view of the house.

"The place is swarming with police", he whispered to himself.

It had not taken too much of his limited brain power to realise that something was seriously wrong when the *Shadow* had come running down the steps and leapt into the car. Now it was well and truly confirmed. He crept back promptly and returned to his car the other side of the woods.

"I'll have to keep out of sight", he muttered ruefully. "They'll be on the lookout for this car, that's for sure."

Harry, meanwhile, had been asking around among his 'contacts', of which there were many, concerning the black saloon car, giving them the number plate. Harry was patient; he loved wandering around looking for clues, checking people's drives for any sight of the car. His patience was at last rewarded in the form of one 'Alfie' - Toby's friend who, of course had good reason to remember the car.

"Yeah, saw it the other day. Watched him park it in a drive and then saw him cover it with a tarpaulin sheet. It was definitely the car. Know it any day. Let me know if you need any 'elp, 'Arry"

Harry set off for the address given him by Alfie and on arrival, calmly crept up the drive. He kept well out of sight, making his way round to the back of the house. He looked in through the window. Higgins was sitting in a chair trying to relax, but not making a very good job of it. He was clearly scared, constantly getting up and pacing up and down the room, biting his nails and occasionally going to the front window and peering through the curtains. Harry waited and watched.

The phone rang and Higgins shot out of his seat in alarm, reaching for the phone and then hesitating to pick it up. *Who was phoning?*

Quickly but silently, Harry tried the back door. It was not locked. He crept up to the living room door via the kitchen and pressed his ear against it. He could just hear what was being said. Evidently it was a friend – he could tell by the way Higgins was speaking. In his fear Higgins was relating to his friend his many troubles, explaining without giving too much away – he wasn't a complete fool – that he could be in trouble with the police. A man the police were after had forced him to take him in the car. Then came the words Harry was waiting for.

"I left him in a lay-by near the woods on the main Chester road."

It was obvious he was talking about the unwelcome occupant of his car. Harry could sense the tension in his voice easing, as he shared it with the caller on the other end of the phone. He didn't say any more about him, but that was enough for Harry. He had another lead. He would go and explore the woods on the main road. Maybe he would come across something.

It was getting late, but Harry was a 'night owl' – this was his kind of thing. He loved it! He set off, carrying a powerful torch, which he would use for emergencies only. *Somebody might be watching.* He reached the woods on his bike at a point where it was possible the car might have stopped, judging this by the direction the car would have taken from the mansion. He knew from the words he had heard that he was looking for a lay-by. He came to the first one on the right hand side of the road, the side the car would have been coming down from the opposite direction. He assumed that the car would have stopped on that side, though he couldn't be sure. He searched along the length of it, getting off his bike and shining his torch along the length of it, looking out for tyre marks. *Nothing!*

Undeterred, Harry climbed back onto his bike and continued, returning back to the left hand side of the road and pedalling furiously till he reached the next lay-by, some considerable distance up the road. He threw his bike down onto the grass verge and crossed over. It was a longer lay-by than the previous one, skirted by dense woodland. *A good place to get out and do a disappearing act through the woods-just the sort of thing I'd do.* He felt he could be on to something. He was! Tyre marks were clearly visible at the far end and continued quite a way along as if the driver had stopped suddenly. There were skid marks in the mud.

Of course they could have been made by any car. He looked more closely and found what he was searching for – a set of footprints leading off into the woods. He needed to follow that trail. Maybe someone was just going for a wee – maybe not! He crossed the road and brought his bike over, hiding it inside the woods behind some bushes.

The footprints took him through the woods, but came to a stop by a series of thick bushes. They seemed to enter the bushes – which seemed strange – but then he realised that they came out on the other side. *Perhaps something had been hidden here?* He managed with difficulty to pick up the trail again till eventually he emerged onto a fairly well-used path. It was pretty obvious which way the person had gone, despite the abundance of footprints he now inevitably encountered. He pressed on along the footpath which led him out of the woods and into a quite well-to-do housing estate. Harry knew it quite well – he used to wander round here in the bad old days, looking for easy pickings. He'd been in the habit of trespassing and stealing in that particular area. It was all behind him now, but maybe some of the expertise could be put to good use. *The problem was, where do we go from here?*

Well the only thing to do was to follow his instincts and do some more snooping. He didn't really know exactly what he was looking for. It would be like looking for a needle in a haystack, but he wasn't about to give up. He'd be guided somehow. He began to move from house to house looking for anything suspicious, checking the bins for any items that might give him some sort of lead – anything. He was like a little mouse scurrying up and down drives and pathways of houses, searching for some scrap of food, some tiny crumb of evidence. Occasionally when he heard voices coming from the houses, he peered through cracks in the curtains just in case he could see anything that would give him a lead. He felt a bit guilty about what he was doing, but he told himself it was in a good cause, a vital cause, and he carried on relentlessly.

He'd done one side of the road and now turned his attention to the other side. Up the drive, round the corner – and into the dustbin! Well, not exactly *into* the dustbin. He hadn't seen it as he rounded the corner and he barged straight into it. It teetered on its base and was about to tipple right over and make the most awful clatter. He managed to catch it somehow and prevent what could have been a most unwelcome calamity. He grabbed the lid as well, but could not prevent something falling out onto the floor. Fortunately what fell out was not anything really solid and potentially noisy, but some sort of discarded cloth or item of clothing. He breathed a sigh of relief and picked up the cloth and was about to replace it in the bin, when his heart skipped a beat. To make sure he shone the light of his torch onto it. It was a rather long garment – the sort of thing he'd seen the vicar wear when he'd been to a funeral once. *But then, he stopped and stared. Yes, it was some sort of mud-stained robe and it was a bit like the description James had given him. The Shadow had worn a robe. Could this be his?*

CHAPTER 13

THE CRACK IN THE CURTAIN

Harry sat down by the bin. He'd never seen the infamous *Shadow*, but they had described him and he knew he was looking for someone dressed in a sort of robe. Mind you, presumably he didn't wear it all the time – could be difficult going to the toilet! And in Harry's humble opinion he wouldn't be seen dead in that kind of gear! He smiled to himself; then he began to think seriously about it.

Maybe the lady of the house had discarded an old nightdress? On the other hand - he opened the garment out to its full length – well fancy that, there was a hood on the end. Nightdresses don't have hoods do they? And wait a minute! He looked at the markings on the robe. It had weird images of the moon and the stars woven into it and a strange sort of sign that meant nothing to Harry. It was the one that James had identified at the secret entrance to the underground passageway. His heart was beating even faster now. What if this house was the very house where the mystery man had escaped to?

He stuffed the robe inside his rucksack and crept towards the rear window of the house. There was a light on. The curtains were shut, but there was the slightest crack where the curtains did not quite meet. He moved to the window ledge and raising his head very slowly, he peered through the crack in the curtain. To his disappointment, so slight was the crack that he could only see across the room and to the left, the fireplace. *Frustrating!*

Harry waited and waited and then waited some more. There was some sort of movement in the room and a figure appeared by the fireplace. The figure was *not* wearing a robe, *but was dressed in black! The mystery person moved to face the window. Harry could see a white face mask. Phew!* Whoever or whatever this creature was, from this earth or the planet Mars, kneeling down and uttering strange moaning or humming sounds it appeared to be offering worship to something or someone. His heart began to pump like an express train. He remembered the suit they had found in Duke's den. The weird moaning was reaching a higher pitch and was developing into a rhythmic chant.

So Harry had never actually seen the ghost of Judge Jeffreys – not that he really wanted to, but he thought he had seen him. Then he realised it was only Duke dressed like a tramp with long hair. That was alright – he could live with that. But now he had actually seen these black weirdoes with the white ghostly faces. He'd had enough! He scampered as silently as he could round the corner, down the drive and then shot like a bolt from the blue into the woods. He ran and ran until he had to stop for breath. When he could carry on he sped through the woods, reached his bike, leapt on to it and pedalled like mad down the road till he reached civilization!

He headed straight for Toby's where they had agreed to meet up should he have anything to report. It was after 10 o' clock but the information he imparted was too urgent to wait till the next day. This could be the breakthrough they needed! James contacted Detective Michael on his mobile phone and immediately a squad of police headed for the address given by Harry. They surrounded the building – it was a detached house – and burst in unannounced, only to find the place empty. They questioned the neighbours either side, but they were elderly and hard of hearing. They didn't go out much and hadn't noticed anything unusual. Michael reckoned the house had been chosen rather carefully for that very reason. The detective was absolutely delighted with Harry's discovery of the robe and already tests were being made for finger prints and DNA. Sadly, so far, there was no match in either case.

There was one other piece of encouragement. The house had been abandoned in some haste and in a cupboard upstairs in an attic room they found a computer. On it was a list of names and it was not long before the police were knocking on doors across the town and discovering evidence that the occupants were definitely linked with the *Shadow* and obviously under his spell. This was all helpful, but of course, as the police and especially Michael himself suspected, they did not know who the *Shadow* was. They had never seen his face – no one had. He had slipped away again and time was running out. If he was about to leave the country they did not know who they were looking for – he was just a *Shadow.*

The hunt was on, but for James, Mary and the others, it was back to school. It was hard, in fact, almost impossible to get the thing out of their minds. Lessons seemed to drag on and on, particularly history.

However, they were about to encounter a most surprising turn of events, which put a whole new perspective on history lessons. Hammy announced that an extra after-school lesson was being laid on for some of the History class, to which all the class were invited, indeed any students who were interested in the subject matter. Many staff members would be present as well. It was when the special visiting lecturer was announced that James and Mary looked at each other open-mouthed. His subject was to do with the time when India was part of the British Empire. Some students were making a special study of that period, but it was thought it might be of interest to others.

It was *very* interesting to two students in particular! And when more information was given concerning him, they could hardly believe their ears. The visitor was from India and a native of the country. He had been in the UK for some considerable time, it seemed. James looked at Mary, the potential significance of it all dawning on them both:

"It's got to be him, Mary; surely it can't just be a coincidence. He could be the one – it fits, perfectly. We've got to go to it; maybe this is the last chance to nail him. We'll follow him after the lecture; get the number plate of his car. There must be some way – there has to be." Mary kept nodding excitedly. *It had to be the breakthrough they needed.*

They entered the school hall where the lecture was to take place. Quite a good number of students and members of staff were there and a general buzz and murmur of conversation suggested an air of anticipation. The speaker duly arrived, brought in by Hammy the Head of History who introduced him to a round of applause.

"Hammy's looking pleased with himself", said James, whispering behind his hand.

Hammy now stood up and introduced the speaker, who was very well qualified in his subject and had lectured in many places across the world. The lecture began and he was clearly a very good speaker who knew how to hold an audience almost spellbound. He was definitely a native of India; in fact, he reminded them of the brutal *Thug* whom they had encountered in the mansion. He could have been his twin – perhaps he was! Except he didn't have that cold and callous look to his features and his manner was charming - the perfect gentleman. When James whispered as much to Mary, she replied:

"But that's what he'd want us to think, isn't it?"

The lecturer continued relating his wide-ranging experience and his many lecture tours, including a prolonged period in the United States. This brought more nudges and diggings in the ribs.

The detective had specifically mentioned the USA as one of the places where this vile sect was growing. It had to be him, but how could they prove it? This was always the problem with the Shadow. No one knew what he looked like and they had no proof, no evidence. And yet there he was standing on the platform, as large as life and yet untouchable. The police had examined the robe discovered so brilliantly by Harry but still there was no match for either fingerprints or DNA. The man was a Shadow and they were chasing shadows. It was no use, unless they could get his fingerprints after the lecture. The glass of water – yes!

The lecture ended and James and Mary came out feeling thoroughly depressed. James had gone up to the platform to see if there was any chance of getting hold of the glass of water. It had been brought in by one of the pupils and the speaker immediately picked it up and drank from it. But then, after the lecture Hammy had motioned to the pupil to remove the glass. The boy reluctantly took it from the desk and turning, promptly bumped into an approaching student eager to ask the lecturer a question and dropped it onto the floor. There was a loud crash of splintering glass and the precious piece of evidence scattered into pieces which were then trodden into the floor by the clumsy feet of passers-by. James put his head in his hands - so near and yet so far!

Hopping from one foot to the other whilst still trying to look inconspicuous, they waited till he came out of the building. At last he emerged, after lots of hand-shakes and expressions of thanks, especially from Hammy, who was positively glowing. They waited for him to go to the car park, where they hoped to get a sight of his car and also its number plate. But he headed for the bus stop just outside the school. The bus arrived immediately, while James was still deciding whether they should board the bus with him. They sprinted out of the school gates, but the bus moved off. It was the usual town centre bus. Ultimately, he could be going anywhere from the town centre. Foiled again!

Standing there, scratching their heads in frustration, they were just about to make their way back to the school yard where their bikes were kept, when two members of staff passed them deep in conversation about the lecturer. Apparently, James gathered, the lecturer had been persuaded by Hammy to come again tomorrow for a second lecture at 10 am. That cheered him up because it meant there might still be another chance. But then, as the two men continued talking, something else was said which at first Bondy didn't particularly take in. Mary had seen a girl she knew well and they were busy chatting away, so she heard nothing of the conversation. The two members of staff had gone past and what they had said was only just sinking in to James's mind. He stood there staring at their retreating forms as they passed out of the school gates. Then he froze on the spot, eyes slowly growing wider and wider as it dawned upon him. *Yes, Yes, it could be, it could be!*

Mary was just finishing her conversation with her friend and was turning toward James when he shouted excitedly:

"I'll see you in a minute, wait for me." Then he dashed off at top speed as if he was in one of his four hundred metre races. She saw him disappear into the main building. He was heading for the upper floor where his history classroom was. He shot up the stairs two at a time, nearly colliding with the caretaker – a jovial Pakistani, who knew James well.

"Sorry", he mumbled and then continued racing up the stairs, watched by the smiling caretaker. He entered the classroom. It was empty – he had the place to himself. A few minutes later he emerged with a big grin on his face. He paused at the large window that looked down over the school yard to the car park. Then his smile grew even broader as he watched the cars leaving the car park. Mary was waiting for him in the school yard with a puzzled look on her face.

"Where have you been?" She looked at him suspiciously, noting the big smile on his face.

"Oh I've just been to get something", he replied, "something rather important for my project." He was smiling again in a strange kind of way.

"Shall I see you tonight?" she asked. "Definitely", he replied, with an even bigger smile on his face.

CHAPTER 14

CLOSE ENCOUNTER

The police had been questioning the men and women arrested after the raid on the housing estate and the discovery of the computer. Their questioning of *Thin Man* and the Indian had yielded nothing that could help in catching the *Shadow*. The simple fact was that they, like everyone else, genuinely did not know who he was. They had spoken to him on the phone, but whenever he visited them or addressed a meeting he always wore the mask beneath the hooded robe. Such was his power over them that they never questioned him about anything unless it related to his orders. So they knew practically nothing about his background. They were totally under his spell. He was like some sort of evil High Priest of an evil and ugly cult. What they did gather was that he was using drugs and subtle hypnotic power to control them. They spoke of meetings where the crowd felt overwhelmed by a kind of evil force that they could not resist. Michael was able to testify to the power of that force. He had felt it himself when he had attended the meeting in the park, under cover.

"It was scary, I can tell you", he said grimly. "I know what they're talking about."

Not surprisingly those numerous prisoners from across the town yielded nothing either. After all they had not been as close to him as the other two. It was a dead end again, or so it seemed. *But was there hope from another quarter?*

After the lecture, before James went home, he called at the police station and left something for Detective Michael. He arrived at Mary's on his bike and strode in with a huge smile on his face. Mary pleaded with him to let her into the secret, whatever it was – though she was sure it was to do with the identity of *The Shadow.*

"I want to keep it as a surprise", said James, putting his arm around her affectionately.

"Well", she replied, "I know who it is now, but I'm intrigued as to how you proved it and how you suddenly changed your attitude and dashed off into the school like a madman. What on earth was going on?"

"You'll just have to wait and see", said James; "and besides I haven't actually proved anything just yet."

Later that night after they had all made their way back to their separate homes, James received a phone call from the detective. As he put the phone down, he stood still with a look of satisfaction but also concern on his face. The identity of *The Shadow* was pretty much confirmed and the police would be taking steps to arrest him, but James had the feeling that it was not over just yet.

The next day the pupils moving around the school toward their lessons were surprised to see a police car pulling into the car park. A buzz of excitement soon spread all over the school as the information was passed by word of mouth from one end to the other. Which of the pupils had been in trouble with the police? It didn't happen often, but it had happened before.

Detective Inspector Roberts and Detective Sergeant Michael Clutton, accompanied by two other officers, made their way to the Head Teacher's office. They were shown in and announced, by a flustered-looking secretary, then were greeted by an equally flustered-looking Head Teacher. He rose to his feet, unsure whether to offer a handshake, thought better of it, then responded to the Inspector's proffered hand and mumbled, in a hesitant tone of voice:

"Gentlemen, um Inspector, how can I help you?"

A name was mentioned to him but, looking shocked and confused, he informed them that the person mentioned was not at the school. He had, in fact, rung in early that morning to say he was unwell and would not be able to come. The inspector and the detective looked at one another in dismay and asked the Head to inform them at once if they should hear anything concerning this person. They urged him to keep the matter entirely to himself and after thanking him politely, left the building. They were watched all the way to the car by every student close enough to a window to get a decent view. Their departure through the school gates was accompanied by a loud cheer.

Bondy had decided not to go to school that day, but instead to stay at home to try to do some private study. Somehow he felt that his moment of triumph at the arrest of *The Shadow* was not one to be gloated about. He was just glad that justice was about to be done. So the call he received from detective Michael to the effect that in fact *The Shadow* had done it again and had slipped the grasp of the police, left him stunned and shocked. To his even greater surprise he discovered that despite knowing the identity of the "monster", as Michael called him, their efforts so far had met with failure. He was still on the loose even though they had pursued the obvious courses of action. Of course, they assured him that every available man would be on call for a nation-wide manhunt. Borders were being watched and airports alerted. It was then, as he reflected on the bad news following the phone call, that James had his moment of inspiration, of revelation. *One solitary word entered his mind and turned the light on in the midst of the depressing darkness. Like Archimedes of old he let out a shout of triumph, but it was not the word 'Eureka'; but the word 'treasure'! The Shadow would not leave without the treasure. Bondy was convinced. The man would not be beaten- that was what he was like. His pride, his arrogance would persuade him, even force him to make one last throw of the dice. He must get the treasure.*

It never really occurred to him how dangerous his next step could be; that meeting face to face with *The Shadow* would be the most frightful, the most desperate of courses to follow. He never for one moment thought to pick up the phone and tell the police where he was going or better, to advise them of his new insight into the situation and let them use their know-how and vast manpower to trap the beast in his lair. There was something in James that responded to such challenges with the deep inward cry of the huntsman, indeed like some hunting hound; its tail up, its ears back, straining to surge forward at the word of command. *The Shadow had to go for the treasure and Bondy had to go for The Shadow.* Like iron filings to a magnet, something in Bondy had to meet head on with something in his adversary.

James was no plastic kind of saint; he was aware of his weaknesses and his failures; he felt fear, he struggled with tensions in his young life – he often got it wrong. But he knew that there was a war going on, not just with guns and weaponry. There were forces of evil that had to be reckoned with. He also knew that the power of God was real and despite his own failings that power was working in his own life. It was rooted in love, truth and righteousness and in the end, love would win.

There was no time to lose. He was in his casual clothes and so without more ado, he dashed out of the house, grabbed his bike and pedalling furiously down the lane, set off for the showdown he felt was certain to take place. Strangely, he was not afraid; a verse from the bible gave him courage and strength: *If God be for us who can be against us?* It didn't really occur to him that he was on his own. He didn't feel he was on his own. He felt that this was a contest between light and darkness – and there was only one winner! His heart was pounding like a hammer and yet within him there was a great calm.

He reached the Four Dogs gateway and shot between the gates and up the drive to the spot where they had gained entrance into the secret cellar.

The place had not been cordoned off by the police. No one knew of it except Bondy & co, the police and the criminals who had now been arrested. Of course, *The Shadow* knew! Two policemen had been posted to guard the spot, keeping under cover in the nearby trees. They were still hidden in the trees, but lying prostrate, face down on the ground. James gasped with horror as he realised they were dead. He knew not how, for there was no sign of violence. A shiver ran through his body. Perhaps he should have turned back at that point, but he could not.

He glanced down at the place where the stone slab with the Druid sign had been. It had previously been replaced and covered up by the police, but it had been removed again! Remembering the struggle he, Toby and Mary had experienced, James could only guess at the strength it must have taken to remove that stone – strength surely more than human. Again, he shivered at the thought. He was aware through Michael, of the powers claimed by this cruel twisted man. He squeezed through the gap and found his footing on the ancient stone steps. Cautiously, stealthily, he began his descent.

Arriving at the place in the wall where he had previously found the second Druid sign, he paused, catching his breath, peering through the gap and listening for any sounds. He could hear nothing except the steady drip, drip of the water down the wall and from the ceiling. Pressing on gingerly, he reached the archway into the main room of the cellar where the boys had been digging for the treasure. *All was quiet.* Rounding the corner, he stepped silently into the room; once again lit up by the seven large candles – *then he saw him!*

He was looking at a piece of paper and staring round the walls of the dark cellar. In addition to the candle-light he also had a large torch. His large staring eyes were scouring the walls so intently he was totally unaware of the presence of the intruder. James was puzzled, for it seemed as though he had the missing piece of the manuscript. That was the only explanation for the way he was looking so intently round the walls. He recalled the words of the peculiar rhyme passed on to them by Granny:

To those who lived within the hall
The key was hidden in the wall.

If you can count to sixty three
A sign within its heart you'll see.

How had he got hold of the information? He was sure Granny had told him nothing. He had implied as much just before they had burst into the room and rescued Granny from their clutches. James wondered if he had solved the mystery of the rhyme. It didn't look like it.

At that moment the man's body stiffened as if somehow he had just sensed the presence of someone in the cellar. The large staring eyes turned towards where Bondy was standing, lost in his thoughts about the mysterious rhyme.

"Ah, so it's you!"

His voice startled James and for a moment he lost focus. Then those large staring eyes seemed to grow even larger and to swell out towards him with piercing and hypnotic power. Bondy blinked his eyes and tried to gather his thoughts and his focus again. The voice continued:

"You've been something of a nuisance, but now perhaps you can be of some assistance to me. I gather your study of the Druids has evidently stood you in good stead. You recognised the sign. Clever aren't you? But, you see; I must get this treasure, it is rightfully mine – my inheritance really. I assure you, when I have it I shall disappear again and perhaps cause you no further trouble – that is if you cause me no further trouble."

"I can't guarantee that", replied James, "and anyway, how can I possibly help you and why should I? You have done so much evil."

He laughed; a hoarse, strangled kind of laugh. "Come now, surely you would love to find this treasure. You could share in its benefits and join me in a purpose the like of which has not been pursued in your life time or even mine."

James made no reply, but simply stood his ground. After a pause, the man looked round the walls again:

"What do you think this means, then, when it says that the key is hidden in the wall and 'count to sixty three'. You're a bright lad aren't you? Come on, why not do it, just for the fun of it?"

James grew bolder, in spite of the weakness he felt in his legs and the fact that his head was swimming. The invisible presence of evil was palpable and he knew he had to make a stand.

"I won't help you or cooperate because I have come here to stand against you and your evil power."

"I see, it's like that is it?" he said taking a step towards James. "In that case I will have to take off the kid gloves. I'm sorry it has to come to this and you will soon be sorry too!"

He raised his hands in the air and then pointed them directly at Bondy, fixing his evil snake-like eyes upon him as he did so. Bondy felt the hair on the back of his head begin to stand on end, his head began to swim so much that it was hard to focus on anything and his legs now felt so weak, he could hardly stand. He thought he was going to faint, then he did, as he slumped against the wall and collapsed in a heap.

CHAPTER 15

LIGHT AND DARKNESS

James woke to find himself being kissed gently and lovingly on the lips. Mary was holding him in her arms, cradling his head and beaming down upon him. Slowly he became aware of bodies moving around him. Uniformed police were escorting someone, handcuffed between two especially burly specimens of law and order. It was *The Shadow,* looking, he thought, with as much of a smile as he could muster; a mere 'shadow' of himself. What had happened? He could not remember. Mary had to enlighten him when he had come round enough to take it in.

"I guessed where you were", she said with a knowing smile. "I just knew it!"

"You know me better than I know myself", he said, smiling gently back at her.

Mary had known that James was at home doing private study. She was at school waiting for the moment when the police would arrest the expected Indian visitor. She was excited when the police arrived, only to be utterly mystified when they left empty handed. Later she heard that the Indian lecturer had not turned up and that he was supposed to be unwell. *I don't think! He's slipped the net again, but how did he know the police were coming?*

She decided to find out from Bondy what he knew about all this. She phoned his house and discovered to her surprise that he was not in. His mother simply said: "Well you know what he's like, Mary. He just went tearing out of the house after he'd had a phone call from the detective. As to where he is – your guess is as good as mine!"

Mary guessed right. The detective must have told him how the Indian lecturer- alias *The Shadow* had gone missing again. It didn't take her too long to guess what Bondy's thinking might be. *The Treasure!* But then her stomach turned over at the thought of Bondy facing that brutal monster alone. She set off immediately on her bike, heading for the secret entrance to the underground cellar. The heavy stone covering the entrance had been removed – somebody must be in there. Then she saw the two lifeless bodies of the policemen. She gasped in horror and panic set in as she thought of Bondy all alone. She began to make her descent, taking care not to slip or make any scraping noise with her feet. Bondy must be down there. *The Shadow* must also be there. As she approached the main candle-lit cellar she heard voices, one of which was Bondy's. The other she could not recognise – it sounded peculiar. Then it went very quiet – it was an evil quietness that made her feel ill-at-ease. *What was going on?*

She was unsure about proceeding further, but felt she just had to. Reaching the entrance to the main cellar, she peered round the corner of the wall. To her utter dismay and horror, Bondy was lying prostrate on the floor, obviously completely unconscious – or worse! *No, she could see he was still breathing. Thank God!* She looked up to see the other occupant of the room. He had his back to her, staring at the walls with a piece of paper in his hand. It didn't look like the Indian, mainly because he was not wearing a turban, or that weird high priestly sort of get-up. In fact he was wearing a suit.

Then something strange happened. The evil, oppressive quietness, awakening fear and dread, gave way to a new kind of silence which began to fill the place. It was awesome and yet peaceful, awakening not dread, but reverence, love and a desire to worship. She felt like kneeling down. After a pause, she did kneel down.

But at the very moment that this sense of *Presence* filled the room, the figure standing at the far end spun round with a cry of anguish. He seemed at first to be looking at Mary. But then she realised he was not looking at her but at some point immediately behind James as he lay helpless on the floor.

The wide staring eyes of *The Shadow* stood out from their sockets, not with evil, sneering dominance over his prostrate victim, but with wild terror and horror. He covered his face with his hands and dropped to the floor, screaming in a kind of agony.

Mary could see nothing immediately behind James. She didn't really need to see anything, for she knew for sure that the evil figure, now cringing on the floor, *had* seen *Someone* standing behind Bondy's prostrate body. He had seen Jesus Christ in some sort of vision, standing over Bondy and the sight had hit him with such force that he could not stand and was filled with terror. She had never seen a vision herself, but she had felt that same presence in her own life and she recognised it.

Mary recognised something else which totally staggered her. The man lying cringing on the floor, the man who was clearly *The Shadow* whose identity they had sought so long, was not the mysterious Indian lecturer; *it was Hammy, her history teacher! Mr Hamilton, Hammy Hamster! How could it be? And what had happened between him and Bondy?*

Slowly she rose to her feet, still conscious of the overwhelming and yet wonderful mystery of the moment. Taking out her mobile phone, she rang the direct number they had been given to reach the detective. Only minutes later the police sirens could be heard and soon after, footsteps pounding down the cellar steps. Michael burst into the cellar gasping for breath and looking extremely anxious. He stopped in his tracks as he surveyed the incredible scene. Then instinctively, he crossed himself – it seemed the right thing to do, though he was not a religious man.

By this time Mary was kneeling beside James and administering her own particular brand of first-aid. It was proving very effective! So when the detective asked her, with a worried look on his face:

"Is he okay?"

She replied with a beaming smile and a blush: "Yes, he's fine."

Turning to the other person bowed down on the floor with his head in his hands, uttering low animal-like noises, he shook his head in disbelief: "I can't believe it. What did James do to him?"

"He didn't do anything", said Mary, her eyes shining with gratitude and joy as she held James in her arms. "No doubt he'll tell you about it later and do you know what? I can't wait to hear the whole story myself."

CHAPTER 16

EXPLANATIONS

James was soon back on his feet and raring to go again. The four youngsters were united with their families again, chastened and no doubt much wiser after their cruel captivity. Granny was well on the way to recovery after his terrible ordeal and was beginning to enjoy being pampered by the nurses in the hospital. He was delighted and relieved to find out how things had worked out and a visit from his friend in the History Society had yielded some further information. He was able to tell them how Hammy, alias *The Shadow,* had found the last piece of the jigsaw relating to the treasure. After all no one suspected Mr Hamilton the history teacher, so when he requested the information – for his research – it had been given him. Granny's friend had no idea about Granny's desperate situation and it never occurred to him to query the validity of the request.

The main topic of interest on all sides, when the friends gathered at Toby's house was: *How on earth did Bondy solve the mystery of the Shadow's identity?* They were joined by a delighted Detective Michael Clutton and, much to Toby's delight, Carol came too.

"Take us back to that moment in the school yard", said Mary. "You know, when you suddenly seemed to grasp something and shot off into the school building."

James smiled, knowingly, looking up at the ceiling as if he was experiencing it all over again.

"It's so simple really. As we were walking across the school yard a couple of teachers passed us and were talking about the lecture by the Indian – who was then our real suspect. They commented on the fact that Hammy seemed to know him quite well. They also said that they had discovered that Hammy had actually been born in India – of English parents of course. My ears pricked up when I heard that, I can tell you – especially when they went on to say that they had heard Hammy conversing with him in Hindi. He could speak the language! Then it hit me like a flash of lightning. When we were listening outside the door of the room where they were holding Granny and that *Thug* was performing his horrible ritual with the scarf, I had recognised two voices in the room. One was, of course, dear old Granny and the other was the dreaded *Thin Man;* but there was another voice and somehow it seemed familiar, though I could not see how at the time. But when I heard what the two teachers said about Hammy, it dawned on me – unlikely or even impossible as it seemed – *it could be Hammy!* What a cover! No wonder we couldn't work it out! It was Hammy all the time."

"But what was it you went to do in the school?" asked Mary, leaning forward in anticipation.

"I dashed up the stairs to the History room and there on the desk as usual, were his spare spectacles in their case.

I grabbed them quickly – in my handkerchief of course – and ran back down to the yard."

"He called at the Station with them and we were able to match the fingerprints with the ones on the robe discovered by Harry and others found in the room at the mansion." Michael was smiling as he spoke.

Then he turned and looked at Bondy with a puzzled expression on his face: "However, what I'd like to know is what really happened in that cellar when you were face to face with *The Shadow*? Now that *is* a mystery to me."

James met his gaze, lowered his head, as if in deep thought, then lifted it again and looked once more at the detective.

"To be honest Michael, it's a mystery to me. I'm not really sure what happened, especially after I passed out. All I can say is that the history teacher we laughed at and joked about, turned out to be quite the opposite of what we thought. His face was transformed when I told him I would not cooperate and that I had come to stand against him and all he stood for. There was this horrible, indescribably evil, power, sort of emanating from him, through his eyes in particular. It knocked me for six. I hardly knew where I was or what was happening. I felt as if I was passing out and although I fought against it, eventually I did – I just don't remember."

He stopped speaking for a moment, as if he was re-living it all. Then he continued: "You know, throughout this struggle, we've prayed because somehow we knew we were not fighting a physical or even a mental battle. We were sure that there were spiritual forces involved, dark forces – not just the fictitious ones made up in stories or on the screen for people's entertainment. We know people in our church who were once in the grip of these sorts of things, so we knew they were real. But thankfully, we also knew that the power of God through Jesus Christ was greater than all these forces and through Him they could be overcome."

He lowered his head again and paused for breath. When he raised it once more, they could see there were tears in his eyes. The room was silent; you could have heard a pin drop – only the sound of the ticking clock disturbed the breathless hush of the room.

"Before, I passed out", he continued, looking across the room at Mary, "I just remember speaking out the name of Christ silently in prayer. And that's it, I don't know any more, but I think Mary will be able to tell you." He ran his hand across his face wiping away the tears, as Mary came across and put her arm around him and continued the story.

"When I came in, I saw James slumped on the floor. I thought he might be dead. I felt so afraid and I could feel that awful sense of evil power. Then I saw that James was breathing. I was about to go to him when I suddenly realised someone else was in the place. I looked up expecting to see that Indian. We thought it was him, you see – that he was *The Shadow*. He had his back to me staring at the walls, presumably trying to find out where the treasure was. Then he suddenly turned round and I thought it was because he sensed that I had come into the cellar. His eyes began to stare and I thought at first that he was looking at me. Then I realised it was Hammy and he was looking past me to a spot behind where James was lying."

She paused, struggling to control her emotions; then she began again: "That's when I felt this wonderful sense of peace and love and goodness, and I suppose, holiness, really. There's no other word for it – I just wanted to kneel down and worship. In fact I did – beside James, cradling his head in my arms." She waited before continuing, staring into space as she recalled the reaction of Hammy following this wonderful peace.

"He started screaming, this horrible, high-pitched screaming!"

She was speaking much more quickly now and her eyes lit up in a sense of awe, as the scene unfolded again before her.

"He was pointing at *Someone*, who must have been standing behind James. Someone I could sense, but not see, though he clearly could. It had to be Jesus. And he was screaming: *No, not you, not you!* Then he dropped to the floor and lay there sobbing. That's when I phoned you Michael – not because I was afraid, for I was so peaceful, in spite of that horrible outburst. Somehow I knew that whatever that evil force was in *The Shadow,* it had been overcome."

Once more, the room was silent and it was some time before anyone spoke. Typically, it was Harry who spoke, in his own inimitable, priceless way.

"It's God innit? S'obvious innit? He's bigger than anything – no contest!"

And after that, funnily enough, there were no more questions.

CHAPTER 17

BURIED TREASURE!

The only question that did remain was, of course, the treasure. Exciting as its appeal might be, it paled into insignificance in comparison with the sense of achievement they all felt at the victory over the evil that had threatened them, their community and their country. It would be wrong to downplay the importance of the difference one person or group of persons can make when they take action for goodness, justice and truth. Evil can spread like a wildfire from a mere spark, but also in a different way goodness can grow almost irresistibly from a small seed sown, like the acorn that produces the mighty oak tree.

But the treasure could hardly be ignored! It had played such a powerful motivating role in the mind of the elusive *Shadow*. Indeed you might say it had also been crucial in bringing about his downfall. The lust for power is a two-edged sword – it cuts both ways. Hitler's lust for power, beginning in a humble beer hall in Munich, drove him on to strive for world domination, but it also drove him into the Russian winter and the ultimate defeat of his armies.

However, the treasure itself was not evil; perhaps it could be found and become a source for good? They had to find out.

So it was that one night Bondy and his friends, joined by the detective, set out for the underground cellar that had played such a significant part in their lives. The secret entrance close to the *Four Dogs* gateway had now been sealed off, so they made their way through the mansion house, led by the detective who had a key to the premises. Once in the long passageway, they hurried along by torchlight, anxious to reach the scene of Bondy's final triumph.

They lit all seven candles to give themselves as much light as possible and stood in silence gazing round the damp cellar walls. Somehow it seemed the last place you would expect to find a treasure. It was surely a far cry from the exotic locations often seen by them in films in sun-drenched lands across the sea. This place was just dirty, damp and rather smelly!

"Where do we start?" James broke the silence at last, his voice echoing from the dreary cellar walls. He pulled out the letter from Granny which had the rhyme written on it.

"Read it out loud." Mary's voice rang out in the silence.

To those who lived within the hall
The key was hidden in the wall.
If you can count to sixty three
A sign within its heart you'll see.

"Okay, so the key is somehow hidden in the wall, whatever that means", said Toby, shining his torch around the dimly lit stonework.

"What's this about counting to sixty three?" Michael was gazing around the walls hoping for some sort of clue.

Again silence enveloped them as they wrestled with the mystery of it all. James was looking at a point half way along the main wall which stretched unbroken from the wall with the archway of the tunnel entrance. It was the wall that stood on the same side as the site of the old hall – now of course no longer in existence - the same side as the secret entrance that they had found. That made sense, he thought, you'd expect it to be nearer to the old hall itself. He kept looking at the wall, shining his torch all along it, up and down and across. He stepped back a pace or two, rather like an Art specialist standing back to see something in a painting that wasn't evident from close range.

"I think I can see something", he said excitedly.

They all crowded round him trying to make out what he was looking at. "Look", he said, "in the centre of the wall, there's a sort of pattern. You can see it better if you stand back a bit. It's as if something has been added to the original wall. And look", he was pointing excitedly; "look, I can see a pattern, forming a rectangle, sort of standing on its head!" He counted the stones; "Seven across the bottom and nine up – that's it, nine by seven, nine sevens are sixty three! That's got to be it. *If you can count to sixty three.*"

"A sign within its heart you'll see", continued Mary.

"Where is the sign, then?" said Toby.

"Does it mean that the sign is at the end of the line at stone number sixty three?" The detective was now warming to the task.

"What sort of sign will it be?" asked Harry.

"I'm sure we'll know when we see it", said James.

They shone their torches all the way along the top line and especially on the last stone at the top. Then they wondered if it should be the last stone at the bottom and anyway it actually depended where you started from when you counted. That would decide where stone number sixty three was. They searched all those options and Toby was just about to offer his broad shoulders for Bondy to climb up to get a better view of the top stones, left and right side, when James shouted out:

"I think I've got it!" Then he waved the paper with the rhyme on to get their attention, before reading it again and especially the last line:

A sign within its heart you'll see.

"That's it –"within its heart", the heart, the centre of the rectangle. So it'll be the centre stone – four lines up and three lines across."

They all crowded round quickly doing the maths and finding the central stone. But they still couldn't see anything. Then Harry pushed through from the back holding in his hand a scruffy piece of rag:

"'Ere Bondy use this. It's what we gagged them two bullies with. Maybe it will 'elp us again, 'cos I bet that stone could do with a good wipin'."

Bondy grabbed the rag and stretched up to the centre stone. A few firm wipes and: "There's something here – yes, it's one of those Druid symbols, like the one at the secret entrance. This must be it!"

"Press it. Press it", they all cried together. He pressed it, pushing hard with both hands. There was a kind of creaking and groaning as the wall seemed to turn in upon itself revealing an inner alcove behind the wall. They all stood open-mouthed, staring in disbelief into the darkness. Swiftly, they directed their torches down into the dark alcove. Inside, they could see what could only be described as a large ancient-looking chest, complete with metal bands wrapped round it in two parallel strips across its width. It was like the sort of thing that pirates and treasure hunters always found in the films. *So there really was a treasure! But what was in it?*

They stood once again in silence – almost in fear. There were too many dark associations with this treasure: *The Shadow, the Thin Man and even the ghost of Judge Jeffreys. Dare they open it? What would it reveal?*

Surprisingly there was no lock on the chest. It would be easy enough to open, it seemed, but was there some sinister trap awaiting them? They looked at one another, then back at the chest, then back at one another.

"It's got to be you Bondy", said Michael, the others nodding in unison.

Bondy looked at them all, questioningly, starting to open his mouth to protest; then thinking better of it. He turned his attention back to the chest, took a deep breath and began ever so slowly to open the lid. It creaked loudly – almost groaned – as if a human voice was speaking from within, then it gradually fell back, this time with an eerie kind of sigh, till finally it lay completely open to their view. Once again silence reigned, but this time it was a more peaceful silence, as if the chest was relieved to be open at last and its secret revealed. They were staring into the chest with open mouths and gasps of astonished surprise and puzzlement.

The chest at first appeared to be completely empty – except for one thing! At the base of the chest was a mirror and in the mirror the reflection of all their faces as they looked down. There was actually one more object, just below the mirror – an ancient looking scroll. James reached out instinctively and grasped it.

"Read it!" Mary could not contain her excitement.

James unrolled the scroll as they all watched, spellbound, waiting for the next twist in the tale of the mysterious treasure. He shone his torch onto the scroll while they all hastily gathered round him, peering over his shoulder as he read out loud the following words written in old-fashioned script, like something from an ancient bible.

So now you have the treasure found
Go forth my friends and look around
Beyond the darkness and the sin
Beyond the mask and look within

Your face you see and wonder why
But lo, the mirror does not lie
Can it be so, can it be true?
That treasure may be within you?

Remember what He said:
"The Kingdom of God is within you"

The sound of the water drip, drip, dripping down the walls echoed loudly in the profound silence that followed. It was a long time before anyone spoke. It was Harry, grinning all over his face, who broke the silence:

"S'obvious innit? That's the real treasure innit? You know, God inside you! Brilliant, 'nough said!"

There was a long pause as they all took in the simple yet deep, truth of Harry's words. Michael put his arm round Harry in appreciation of the wisdom on such young and uneducated shoulders.

"You're right Harry and I guess we can all learn from that, but what would *Hammy the Shadow* have made of it all if he'd discovered his 'treasure'?"

"Well, I suppose he'd have been blazing mad with frustration and probably cursing God. Or, who knows, maybe he'd have come to his senses and realised that his dream of worldly wealth and power was a false dream. He might have looked at himself and seen the deceit, the lies, the evil inside him and taken off his mask and faced the truth. Perhaps even he might have realised that there is a real, though different kind of treasure and he could discover it, if he was willing." Mary looked solemnly at them all.

Toby nodded in agreement and added: "It mentioned a mask, which I guess we all wear to cover up and hide; but boy, did *he* wear a mask! We didn't know who he was and I don't think he knew himself. I suppose if we're honest, we often don't face up to ourselves. We hide behind a mask. With me, it was being tough. With others it's being respectable on the outside, without facing what we're really like on the inside. It's about facing the truth really. And Jesus said 'The truth shall make you free.'"

There was another pause as they all looked down to the ground, lost in their thoughts. Then James broke in:

"What's the point of gaining the world and losing yourself? Why try to build your own selfish kingdom and fall short of God's kingdom of love? We don't have to search here and there; we just have to get past the rubbish and rubble inside each one of us. Take the mask off, stop pretending and we find God isn't a million miles away. He's right there."

"Yeah", said Harry, "S'obvious, innit?"

They stood in the silence. No one spoke, no one moved. From somewhere a gentle breeze stirred the flames of the seven candles and for a moment it was as if a fleeting shadow passed over each one of them. But this was no evil shadow. The night of the evil *Shadow* had passed and in its place the shadow of a divine presence hovered over them. They all bowed their heads. It seemed the natural thing to do. And then, after a period of total quietness, in which time seemed to stand still, without a word they walked together down the dark tunnel. They left behind the house where they had faced so many dark horrors and stepped out with peaceful hearts into a night that was ablaze with the glory of a full moon – God's faithful witness in the sky.

The *Night of the Shadow* really was over.

Lightning Source UK Ltd.
Milton Keynes UK
UKOW04f0921200315

248208UK00003B/5/P